SEVEN BRIDGES

a novel by
GLENN T. WRIGHT

All rights reserved.

Copyright © 2013 – Glenn T. Wright.
No part of this book may be reproduced or transmitted
in any form or by any means without permission in writing
from the author.

All of the characters and events in this book are fictitious,
and any resemblance to actual persons, living or dead, is
purely coincidental.

Published by the author.
www.glenntwright.com

ISBN-13: 978-1452811680
ISBN-10: 1452811687

SEVEN BRIDGES

Dedicated to my daughters,
Amber and Heather.

Prologue

"How long?" the pilot asked. "How long has she been like this?"

"She's been out for six days." The attending nurse turned to the cockpit, then back to her patient, Leah Goforth.

Motionless, Leah was strapped to a gurney. Sensors clipped to her fingers provided the only signs she was alive—bold green lines moving across a monitor. Slow, her pulse was steady, as were her other vitals, but Leah was away, gone—she couldn't hear the chopper's engine, or see the rooftop of the hospital below.

Covered with fresh snow, frozen plains swept through the landscape of her mind. Westward—away from the brutal hands that had caused her to seek sanctuary in a dream—she took cautious steps. Watchful, she knew that scenarios, like people, can sometimes change in an instant.

Somewhere, over the rainbow... Humming, Leah wished that she, like Dorothy, had a home she wanted to return to, but she didn't. Hers had become a house of pain, a life of cruelty and persecution. Not even her love for Elijah, her twin, could prevent the coma she'd willed herself into.

Where am I? She wondered why this strange deserted place was her mind's choice for refuge. *Just keep going. Keep moving.* It didn't matter where she was, as long as she continued to distance herself from the past. *Keep going.*

Drawn to white-crested peaks in the distance, she hurried. *Maybe the Emerald City's up there in those hills!*

He'd never been away from home, much less in a helicopter. With a cheek near the glass, Elijah Goforth viewed the mountains of West Virginia. Frightened, his thoughts were as scattered as the leaves below. *She'll come back,* he thought. *She'll come back. She has to.* He looked at Leah through the corners of his eyes.

"Everything alright?" the nurse asked.

Avoiding eye contact, he stared through the window, then turned again to his sister, who was covered with sterile sheets. He wanted to shake her, and to keep shaking until she came back. But he didn't. No. He understood her reasons.

Practiced at trying to be invisible, he kept his face near the window, and, to the relief of the transport team, he was silent throughout the flight.

"Inbound, we have visual. Descend from the north."

"Copy," the co-pilot answered, looking below, where a large white X marked the landing zone.

Atop a red brick building that blended into the Vermont countryside, Meadowsview's trauma team awaited the arrival of their new patients and quickly moved Leah onto a wheeled bed.

Elijah unbuckled his belt, then reached below his seat. With his only possession, a small wooden box, held close, he grasped a hand that guided him from the helicopter onto the rooftop.

"You must be Elijah." The staff psychologist smiled, trying to ease the fears of the nervous child. When he tried to release her grip, she forcefully held his wrist. "I'm Annie," she said. "Your sister's going to be fine. She'll be fine." She led him to an elevator. "Three," she said. "Your room is on three. Do you know what the number three looks like?"

He remained silent, then raised his left arm. Confused and scared, Elijah was doing his best to stay calm. He glanced at his box, at Annie, and finally pressed the button for the third floor.

A bed. A dresser. A nightstand. A lamp. It was larger than the room he'd been in for several days, and this one had something the other one didn't—a table on which were boxes of markers, crayons, and pencils, more than he'd ever had at home.

He walked to the table and picked up a clean white

sheet of paper, then took a single gray pencil from a box.

Sitting on a plastic chair, his concentration was immediate. He gripped the pencil as his left hand twitched. Spasms shot through his arm, but quickly subsided.

With several strokes of the graphite tip, the outline of a covered bridge was complete. Clouds. Trees. The elements fell into place as Elijah shut the world out and did the only thing that made sense. He drew.

Dr. Kathleen Scott took a deep breath before entering his room. His admission exam the day before had ended in a tantrum. Stepping inside, she braced herself for another meltdown. But this time was different.

Focused on the page in front of him, he made no eye contact or acknowledgment of her presence.

She quietly watched, wondering if anyone would ever break through the invisible shell around him.

"What's that you're working on?" she finally asked, not expecting an answer. The only thing she was sure of was that he had nothing to say to her. She watched for a few minutes, looking occasionally at his file in an effort to appear less obvious.

Finally, she went to the door. Gripping the knob, she briefly faced him.

"A dream," he whispered, not looking up from his drawing.

She stood frozen. He'd never spoken directly to her. Not like this.

"A dream?" Kathleen released the doorknob. "Is that

what you dreamt last night?"

"No," he responded, clenching the pencil tighter. "Not *my* dream..."

"Whose?" She stepped forward, hoping for an answer that didn't come—he'd already retreated into the safe, familiar silence.

With eyes wide open, she stared at his drawing as Elijah gazed through the window, unmoved by the colorful autumn morning.

Chapter 1 – David

I dreamt of another time and another place. A pristine beach with pure white sand. An island in the South Pacific.

You might think that my sleep was restful, soothing, and you'd be partly right. But I awakened to sheer emptiness, wanting only to close my eyes and return to the time before the word 'regret' had any true meaning to me.

At thirty-one, I felt like I was two different people. There was the professional side, whose research into paranormal dream states was well-respected. Then there was the private me, the one whose weekends were spent in Hollywood nightclubs. To phrase it mildly, the two sides were at odds, conflicted.

The last year had been especially difficult.

Before my trip to Lauani, I'd usually managed to stay a glass away from complete inebriation, but after returning things were different. *I* was different, and 'oblivion' was one of the few places I found any true measure of solitude.

My career had taken off, and I was thankful. But the rigors of a demanding schedule—combined with my excessive drinking—had taken an emotional toll. Anxiety. Depression. I was a walking head case, a psychologist in need of a psychiatrist.

Their soft scent, mysterious nature, and off-the-wall way of thinking drew me to some women, but I really didn't see myself as the kind of guy someone would take home to meet mom and dad. If one suggested it, I cringed at the prospect and soon became "David Weston—the guy who never called back." And so my private life was limited, as I never seemed to be committed enough, or attentive enough, or a hundred other adjectives describing my inability to sustain a relationship. After several failed attempts, I gave up on meeting anyone who would really put up with me, then began a period of frequently waking up beside a complete stranger, wanting only for her to get dressed, grab her bag, and go. 'Long term' was when she was still there in the afternoon.

Of course, I'd convinced myself that my habits were no worse than anyone else's, which made it easier to continue down my path of self-destruction.

Most of my friends were noted professionals too, and

we met at the trendiest clubs and restaurants, wearing the latest look, eager to show off our new cars, jewelry, and symbols of our status. Always the loudest table, appearing to be having the most fun, we were quick-witted, all-knowing, ever-impressive bar closers, and life was sweet. But for me, somewhere along the way the sports cars lost their luster, and the house on a hill provided only so much enjoyment. It seemed like there had to be more. And though I sometimes saw the same restlessness and discontent in the eyes of my friends, I smiled and tried to give the impression of complete happiness. Besides, there was my work...

In my stacks of research, were pieces of puzzles, clues to mysteries, answers.

The Island Files, while hard to view, provided an abundance of data, yielding priceless support for my statements. With many hours of digital recordings, these files were the focal point of my studies on lucidity. And it was these files that led to the realization that there are some things we're better off not understanding.

Some of my discoveries were disturbing, but one thing, the story I'm about to tell you, changed me in ways for which I wasn't prepared.

"Thought transference?" I'd heard the words and seen the accompanying sneers so many times that I'd come to expect them. But after the publication of my third book, which drew heavily from my experiences on the island, I was propelled from being virtually unknown to having a rigorous agenda. Surprisingly well-received, my research caught the attention of many of the right people, and I began receiving invitations to speak at nearby colleges. I hated it at first. All eyes upon me as if I were a guru or dream decoder with all of the answers.

Overwhelmed by the changes, I was lucky to have Kelli handling my business relations. She capably dealt with my calendar, and even made it a point to tell me in person that I was to be the Guest of Honor at a formal dinner in late October. "Don't blow this. Be there on time, wear a black bowtie. And David." She paused. "That tie better be on straight." I knew exactly what she meant and trusted her implicitly. And despite my routine, often irreverent, escapes into the LA nightlife, I usually managed to arrive sober and on time to my appointments.

Twice monthly the gardeners could be heard mowing and blowing, and Rosa came Mondays, Thursdays, and, reluctantly, every other Saturday.

"Joven... too much playboy, too much drinking," she said with a Spanish accent.

I scratched my retriever behind the ears. "Don't you have clothes to fold or windows to wash?" I smiled, but knew she was right.

"I don't do windows, no windows, every time I tell you, no windows! Dali, off the couch!" Opening the sliding door, she snapped her fingers and my dog abruptly lifted his head from my lap and ran through the den. "You too, outside. Go play with your dog, I need to clean." She looked me straight in the eyes and ushered me to the door.

It was a Saturday afternoon and my head was

throbbing as I lay on a hammock throwing the well-chewed tennis ball. The previous night had been like too many before. I'd waded through the Hollywood crowds and ever-present paparazzi, all hoping for a glimpse of the latest diva or rapper. But it was all transparent to me, and I entered the clubs like I owned them. Greeting other regulars, John and I kept a watchful eye on the waitresses who fueled us with rum until we headed to the next bar or paired off with party girls. Last night she was a redhead who, after several hours of debauchery, was good enough to call a cab. She left with the proverbial "Call me," but grinned as if to say she wouldn't be waiting by the phone. By the time the taxi left my driveway I'd forgotten her name, managing only to stumble back into my den, where I mixed another drink.

I placed the glass beside the bathroom sink, and when I reached for the faucet, knocked it over. Feeling like an imposter, I stared at my reflection. What would my friends say if they knew the truth? What would they say if they saw my left wrist and the shard with which I repeatedly scratched at a prominent vein? Certainly, last night was like many before, but in the sober light of day nobody knew of the ghost that caused my dark contemplations. Sarcasm hid my private torment, and long sleeved shirts covered the cuts.

Now, viewing the past from a new perspective, I can see that I was hanging by a thread, slowly losing my mind, and had it been anyone else I probably wouldn't have even thought about going. But as fate would have it, it wasn't just anyone, it was Kathleen, and I'd soon board a plane that would lead to much more than absolution.

Startled by its ring, "Hello," I answered my cellphone, having no idea that providence would arrive in this call from an old friend.

"How are you, David?"

"I'm good... wonderful. And surprised... its been a long time." I sat up in the hammock as Dali dropped the slobbery ball beside me.

"Oh, you're not nearly as surprised as I am. I've been trying to reach you for quite a while. Thought you'd fallen off the face of the earth." She hesitated, giving me a chance to respond, then continued, "It's pretty sad that I actually expected to get your voice mail, like the forty times before now. What's wrong, too hung-over to screen calls, or losing your touch?" The silence that followed was almost laughable, but neither of us laughed. I really wanted to say something, anything, but knew that whatever I might say would be short of the truth. So I kept quiet, literally biting my lower lip.

"Look, you owe me a favor. I need you to come to Vermont."

"What's wrong? And wait, why do I owe you a favor?"

"I really can't explain right now, I'm due in a meeting. But trust me, you should be here."

"Actually, I should probably take an aspirin and have a long nap." I massaged my temple. "When?"

"What are you doing tomorrow?"

"Tomorrow? Thanks for the advance notice."

"I don't have time for this right now. But, first of all, *you're* the one who's not taking calls. If you hadn't been avoiding me you'd already know what's going on. Look, there's a flight from Los Angeles to Albany tomorrow morning. Book it and call me before you board." The crucial tone in her voice left no room for indecision, and I knew that I'd go. The time to face her had come.

After only a minute or two of bitching, my brother agreed to watch my dog and take me to the airport, and the next day we were in his SUV on the 105 Freeway with Dali in the back.

Knowing it was annoying, John thumped the wheel to the latest rap. What he seemed to want was a genuine, heartfelt acknowledgment that he was doing me a big favor, but I chose verbal engagement instead.

"What's this you're listening to? My head's throbbing from last night, and just to make a point you play *this*?"

Laughing, "Wuss!" he retorted. "Can't hang with the fellas anymore, huh? Let Johnny play something you can handle." Then, in a most brotherly manner, he inserted a disc with an even more rambunctious beat.

"No, let me turn this off." I glared, challenging him as I held my finger on the power button. Staring through the window, hung-over and anxious, The City of Angels seemed to move by in slow-motion.

"So, how'd it go with that blonde?" he asked as if he might've preferred her to the brunette he went home with.

"She has a tattoo of the grim reaper on her butt."

"No way!" He laughed, and after a pause his entire tone changed. "I've talked to her, ya know?" He knew what I was thinking.

"Kathleen?"

"Yep. She was wondering how you were and why you quit taking her calls."

I wasn't sure how to respond. I couldn't respond. How to answer her inevitable questions had been the only thing on my mind.

"What'd you tell her?"

"What *could* I tell her?" He looked at me with questions. "No one really knows but you. I think it's selfish and lame that you haven't spoken to her, but who am I, right?"

"Next exit." I pointed ahead, avoiding further discussion.

"Look out!" I shouted, to which John tapped the brakes and then pulled to the shoulder.

"What! What is it?" he asked.

"Didn't you see her?" I looked through the mirror on my side, and then over my shoulder through the rear window.

Stunned, "See who?" he said. "Wait. Let me guess—the girl again? This is getting ridiculous, David. Isn't this the third time this month? You need to get some fucking help."

I didn't answer. If the truth was known, it was more like the fifth time—the previous week I'd seen her floating in my pool.

With his usual need for attention, he turned the stereo to full volume as he dropped me off at LAX, and I leaned forward and turned it off again.

"You suck." John pushed the button to open the hatch as I got out. He lifted my luggage, and in a brazen tone asked, "So what *are* you gonna tell her?"

I hugged my retriever, took my bag, and gave him the middle finger.

"Look. I know you're a big badass psychologist and all, but you need to get some help." He looked me in the eyes and took a step closer. "Seriously, David, you won't talk to me, but talk to someone—maybe Kathleen." He threw an arm around my shoulder. "I love you, man. Get some help."

An hour later I boarded the jet, still unsure of what I would say when I saw her.

Immediately picking up the airline's in-flight catalog, I merely nodded at the suit-laden businessman who seemed equally content to sit without conversation. "Rum and Coke," and "Another," were the only words I spoke during the entire flight.

Before passing out somewhere over the vast Midwest farmlands, I thought for a moment that the clouds resembled an armada of sailboats drifting toward the horizon.

We finally landed in Albany, where it was good to stretch my legs en route to the exit.

"David. Over here David," the familiar voice caught my attention. Her mild Southern accent perfectly suited Kathleen's demure style. Confident, refined, with pale white skin, dark hair, and green eyes, she was beautiful, but seemed uneasy, burdened.

With a trepid smile, she hugged me, and we were soon in her car, with hardly a word said by either of us. Pulling away from the airport, she attempted another smile, but seemed remote. "I'm so glad you came—I was afraid you'd change your mind."

"So, you gonna tell me what this is all about?" Having been on a plane for several hours, I was ready to find out why.

"Straight to the point, David? And you always say *I'm* the one who doesn't beat around the bush." Changing lanes, she made eye contact. "Something's happening at Meadowsview."

"Yeah, I've kind of deduced that."

"You've heard of people having the same dream?" She gripped the wheel, awaiting reply. But it seemed rhetorical, so I listened.

"A few days ago we admitted two children. Twins. The girl's in a coma, and her brother's autistic. He hardly ever says anything."

"I've never dealt with autism," I interrupted. "And why's the girl..."

Kathleen cut me off. "May I continue? I mean, do you want me to tell you?"

I grinned. It was good to see the feisty southern girl I'd known. And after flatly shutting me up, she continued.

"Elijah's autistic, but he draws all the time, and his work's amazing."

"A savant?" I asked.

"Yes," she nodded, "an autistic savant." She was certain, and intrigued. "I saw something on TV a few years ago. The boy could play the piano like Mozart, but couldn't tie his own shoelaces. That's what Elijah's like."

"I think I saw that same special. PBS or something. But that's not why you asked me to come..." I faced her. "So why am I here?"

"He *knows* her dreams. I think he knows what she's dreaming." Not one to jump to conclusions, when Kathleen made a statement, you could bet she had a way to prove it. And the reason she called was now clear.

"But why's he's here? Wouldn't he be better off with a family member, or..."

"Their admission paperwork was specific about them not being separated. So we've inherited him along with her."

"How long's she been in a coma?"

"Several days."

"And he draws? What does he draw?"

"Mostly landscapes, and his work's very impressive. I mean, you won't believe the detail in his pictures." Then, as though she was blurting it out, "David, what do bridges symbolize?" she asked.

"Bridges?" I stared through the windshield and drew a deep breath. "Bridges represent... life."

My response only adding to her anxiety, Kathleen drove without speaking for a couple of miles. "Life? That's pretty broad—think you can narrow it down a little?" This was my strong suit and she knew it well.

"Crossings. A continuum. Passages between Heaven and Earth." I answered with conviction. "When we dream of crossing bridges, we seek council with Holiness."

For several minutes, the only sound was that of the tires on the road. I viewed the New England autumn and turned frequently to the face that was still as striking as when I'd last seen her, more than two years earlier. I knew that at some point she'd ask why we'd lost contact, but she chose not to go into it immediately, and I appreciated not being put on the spot. Besides, her attention was clearly elsewhere, and I was still trying to put together a reasonable sounding story for refusing her calls.

"What?" She bashfully smiled in response to my flirtatious gaze—the same gaze she'd seen many times when we were at UCLA. But I never crossed the line with Kathleen. Something always kept us above the complications of a physical involvement. Though she was beautiful and desirable, we were from different worlds. I was a California boy, impudent and still unattached, and she was a career-minded, third-generation doctor, a woman of unquestionable character. I couldn't imagine her becoming only another conquest, and knew that she would never settle for anything less than the full-blown, 'Until death us do part' kind of commitment. Somehow it all equated to our relationship remaining strangely platonic.

The distance I'd flown seemed short compared to the distance between us, and we both knew I was to blame.

In the console between our seats were several CD's, which I thumbed through in search of something to fill the silence.

"Where is it?" I grinned.

"Where's what?" she answered, and began twisting her hair.

"You *know* what," I said, looking through the discs.

"Well, I don't know what you're talking about," she turned on the southern accent.

"Pearl Jam. Don Henley. Vivaldi. Katy Perry..." Her taste in music could only be described as eclectic. With a style of her own, she had a sense of identity. To me, Kathleen was many things. Confident. Loyal. Timeless. Perfectly flawed, she was in her own state of grace.

"Okay. Where is it?" I asked, then I noticed a compartment. "What's in here?"

"My sunglasses," she said, trying to keep me from looking inside. But it was too late.

There beside her shades was the CD I was looking for —Jim Croce's Greatest Hits.

"Uh huh," I laughed. "Thought you were clever." I took the disc from its case and inserted it into the player. Knowing very well that 'Photographs and Memories' was her favorite, "What was the name of that song?" I asked.

Smiling, she turned up the volume and sang along—if you could call it that. She knew the lyrics, but couldn't carry a note if her life depended on it. "*Back to a happier day, when I called you mine...* Funny how you hate this song, but you're the one who put it on..."

For a moment, the uncertainty of life disappeared. It was like old times, before she came to New England and I went to Lauani.

"This is my first experience with autism too. And David, he's so smart. But why would he draw bridges?" she asked, frowning. "It's like everything affects him, and at the same time *can't* affect him. He won't allow it. He's like this little bubble in a big scary ocean." She spoke of Elijah with a shudder in her words, a mix of sympathy and admiration.

"I have no experience with autism, but I do have some with bubbles," I said, trying to lighten things up.

"Don't even go there." Acknowledging my lingering review of her long legs, she rolled her eyes, to which I merely changed subjects.

"Vermont's beautiful." We weren't actually in Vermont yet, but we were close enough, and the landscapes were truly breathtaking. Varying shades of orange, red, and yellow leaves shimmered in the cold autumn sunlight, and unlike the brown, smog-ridden LA Basin, could only have been mixed on God's palette.

"For an incredible percentage of our lives we live in our own subconscious—that's what you said." It was a quote from my last book, showing my hiatus was a distant second to what was going on in the hospital.

"Think about it. You sleep, what, seven or eight hours a day?"

"More like six."

"Okay, that means you're asleep for three months out of every year." I'd always been fascinated by the statistics. "And in those three months you'll have over fifteen-hundred dreams."

"But I never remember my dreams, at least very rarely. I mean, in the last year I've had maybe five dreams I remembered."

"So? You think because you don't remember them they don't take place, or maybe they're insignificant? Let me tell ya Kate, you couldn't be more wrong."

Smirking at the nickname, "I believe you," she said,

and faced me. "At least now I do."

After stopping for gas in Bennington, we rode quietly for a while.

"I had a dream," she said.

"Wanna tell me about it?"

"We're getting close, but yes, I'd like to. Maybe after you're settled in, we can talk over dinner."

Having brought only a carry-on and laptop, I knew settling in would take all of twenty minutes. "Okay, we'll talk at dinner... maybe do some catching up."

As we turned onto another road, "We're here," she said.

I stared at the remarkable structure a quarter mile ahead, wondering what wayward nineteenth century architect had placed a red brick castle in the heart of New England. The building blended perfectly with the dense maples on either side and was cradled by a colorful hill behind it.

"Very nice," I said as we drove through the meadow, about the length of a football field, in front of the hospital.

Noting the number of cars in the large lot east of the building, "Quite a crew, huh?" I added as I opened the back door for my bags.

"Well, we have a good-sized medical staff, therapists, administration, cooks, maids. And this is the weekend. Tomorrow this lot will be packed."

We entered through the main lobby, and the serene, postcard exterior turned into Meadowsview, a noted New

England trauma research facility.

Several staff members greeted us, and Kathleen, always a beacon of manners, politely introduced me. There was never a doubt in my mind that she would succeed in whatever she tried. She was one of those people with an inherent sense of direction, and she'd distinguished herself here in a relatively short time.

We walked through the main hallway and passed a waiting room where a young boy was drawing. I assumed that this was the autistic twin, and the look in Kathleen's eyes quietly confirmed that this was Elijah.

A nurse sat beside him and was speaking, but the boy didn't respond. Emotionless, he sat in an awkward position, flinching often. But with remarkable awareness he'd mastered the ability to simultaneously lift his pencil with each spasm. Entranced, his focus was extraordinary, until the nurse startled him by reaching for a small wooden box. "What's in here?"

Grasping the container, he held it to his chest with a look that said, *"This is mine! Don't even think about it!"* Placing it beyond her reach, he glared through the corners of his eyes before guardedly returning to his work.

We watched unnoticed until Elijah lifted his head and turned to face us. Anguished, his dark eyes seemed to look right through me.

"I'll show you your room," Kathleen said.

On the fourth floor she handed me a room key and visitor's badge. "These are yours." We stopped in front of my door. "Be sure to wear this one til we get your permanent pass." She tugged on a nylon lanyard, showing me her photo-ID. "I'll give you some time to unwind. We can meet at the cafeteria at eight. Okay?"

"Sure." I swiped the key. "That'll give me time for a shower and short nap. But how about nine? Can we make it nine?"

"Alright," she agreed, knowing I was exhausted. "Just be on time. Set your clock."

Leah's nurse turned her from one side to the other and wrapped her hands around the child's knee. To the sound of several monitors, she massaged her patient's leg. Thinking of the dinner she'd promised her boyfriend, she occasionally glanced at the girl she wished would miraculously open her eyes.

But Leah was in another place, far from the sterile room where the staff watched her vitals without expectation. A life of punishment and abuse was far behind her now, and she looked eagerly ahead, to the snow covered mountains which stood out against the dark backdrop of her dream. There, no one could hurt her, and she could walk without fear, far from the brutal hands that caused her to close her eyes and begin this journey. Step-by-step she moved closer to the peaks ahead.

"Oz," she whispered. But, unlike Dorothy, she knew in unthinkable ways that there was no place like home.

At first it was faint, it could've been only the wind. Then it grew louder, closer. She looked quickly to her sides, then behind her.

Calculating. Threatening. The dark horse snorted a

warning. Frost shot from its nostrils as it came closer, coldly staring through soulless black eyes.

Framed black and white photographs of maple leafs were hung on the honey colored walls of my room, which was tastefully decorated with Early American furniture.

Setting my luggage on a chair, I stared through the middle window at the trees across the meadow.

Hot water pounded my stiff shoulders as I stood in the shower for several minutes before taking a towel. After wiping the steam from the mirror, I stared at the circles under my eyes. With pale skin and gray streaks in my dark hair, I looked ten years older than I did a year before then.

Hungry and exhausted, I barely managed to set the alarm on my phone before falling across the bed.

The fourth floor was a dormitory for visitors and several staff members who lived on-site. After exchanging cordial nods with two nurses I'd met when we arrived, I continued to the elevators, still tired but trying my best to appear composed.

Kathleen, always punctual, was waiting in the lobby and led me to the cafeteria. "You're in rare form," she said, "actually on time for a change." With a grin, she continued. "Minor surgery, that's what we call the cafeteria here. It's like our password when we're in front of patients. So if you hear someone say they'll be in minor surgery, it means they're starving. The food really isn't bad though. Fairly edible."

The server politely smiled as she placed a large portion of lasagna next to the warm rolls and Caesar salad on my plate. Tray in tow, I followed Kathleen to a table near the windows.

I always teased her about saying grace. Diners, fast-food joints, fine restaurants, it didn't matter, she always put her hands together and closed her eyes for a moment before each meal. Brought up a Southern Baptist, she was taught to be appreciative of God's gifts. I, on the other hand, was much less devout. As a boy, I attended Sunday School, where I learned more about making paper airplanes than about The Bible. The bus of a nearby church stopped at our house for awhile, but by the time we were in our teens my brothers and I preferred sleeping in. Still, I admired her faith. There was nothing pretentious or less than genuine in her devotion.

"Amen," I said as she opened her eyes.

"It wouldn't hurt you to say a prayer now and then, ya know?"

On the far side of the room, the janitor appeared to be in his mid-twenties. Dreadlocks bouncing, he listened to a headset while repositioning the tables and chairs where he was working. Completely content, he went about his duties with a clear measure of pride, smiling at his reflection in the marble he'd just polished.

"To you, David." Kathleen raised her glass. "I appreciate you coming."

"It's not like I had much of a choice." I tapped mine

on hers. "But I'm glad I came."

Not wanting to go straight into it, she stayed clear of the topic through dinner, and we discussed anything else until we were finished eating.

"Now about your dreams," I asked, followed by a quiet moment when her expression held the same anxiety I'd noticed on the way from the airport.

"Right... my dreams." She glanced at me, then turned to the large window beside our table. "Like I said, I never remember my dreams, not most of them anyway. But I had one the other night, and parts of it were so vivid."

"An important dream," I said, sensing her anxiety.

"It was like I was really there." She stared into the dark meadow. "I was walking through a covered bridge, and there was a misty fog around everything. Someone was on the other side, but something scared me, so I turned around and ran."

"Who was on the other side?"

"Leah. And she was trying to say something."

"What? What did she say?"

"I don't know. But that's just part of it. The next morning, on top of Elijah's nice, neat, tidy little stack, was a drawing of the same damned bridge."

I always smiled when Kathleen swore. It just seemed funny when the sweet southern belle cursed. Completely out of character, it was when I least expected it, and always said as though I was the only one to ever hear her cuss. She was priceless, although not exactly thrilled by my brief amusement.

"I'm glad you find this so entertaining." With a biting glance, she turned back to the window.

Thought devolution was a concept I'd studied extensively, even to the point of visiting a Polynesian island whose inhabitants practiced it in many of their rituals. It was there that my life was forever changed, that I found my greatest discovery, but also left a piece of myself behind. Somewhere on the untouched beach, a part of me was submerged in the eternal tides—an unending Baptism in an ocean that knew my disgrace.

"David?" she asked, her voice striking a strange chord. "Do you believe in God?"

"Wow. Where did *that* come from?" I asked. It seemed like she should've already known. But in all fairness, sometimes even I didn't know what I believed anymore. "Yes, of course," I finally answered.

"I mean, do you really *still* believe in God?" She turned with the assured content of those who know they'll be graced with angelic eternity.

Gazing at her reflection in the window, I wondered if my own eternity would be as gracious.

"Sometimes I thank Him. Sometimes I curse Him. Sometimes..." I shrugged my shoulders. "Sometimes I just wonder if anyone's listening." I glanced at the shirt sleeve covering my left wrist.

She merely nodded as if to say, *Yes. He's listening.*

"How do you know it was the same bridge?" I changed subjects.

"It was," she responded immediately. "Jesus, he drew my dream. What does that mean?"

"I don't know," I answered, reaching across the table

She placed her hand in my open palm. "Sincerely, thank you for coming. I've really missed you."

Flirting with one of the cooks, the janitor paused when we first made eye contact. He closely examined me, and I him. Then he laughed and returned to his work as she threatened him with a spatula.

Chapter 2 – Meadowsview

"I should give you the grand tour," she said.

With no further discussion about her dreams, we put our trays away and began down the hallway.

The second floor corridor was well lit compared to the cafeteria. "This is, well," she nodded behind us, "the cafeteria, of course..." She led to the elevators, where she pointed to several doors at the end of the hall. "And some administrative offices."

The third floor hallway was like stepping into an emergency room, as nurses and doctors, each with a degree of confidence, performed an array of tasks. Clearly, Meadowsview's staff was well-trained, and its notoriety deserved.

At our end of the hall, just past the elevators, was the Records Room. Kathleen pointed to the door. "In there are what we call the 'Dinosaur Files'. All patient records are scanned into our database, so we basically just use the hard copies as backups. I think they're easier to read though, and still pull one now and then." She paused. "David, I'm giving you full access to this room." Her change of tone seemed to suggest that she was hoping I'd discover something important in the files.

"The twins, what's their last name?"

"Goforth," she answered, then glanced at her watch. "But let me finish showing you around. You can look tomorrow."

She then escorted me through Meadowsview.

Captivating, the structure was a combination of antiquity and modern efficiency.

When we passed the nurse's station on the third floor, Kathleen pointed from the counter to the far end of the hall. "The rooms on this side are for the more critical cases, kind of like an ICU." Each of the ten rooms had additional monitoring equipment and a nurse assigned to the bedside.

I quietly followed, admiring her skill as she greeted the nurses and asked about the patients.

At the end of the hall, she stopped and looked through the window for a moment before entering Leah's room, where an intern, appearing to be in her early twenties, was reading a romance novel out loud.

"I hope you're editing the spicy parts, Rebecca," she said.

Blushing, the young woman placed the book beside her, and stood up.

"This is David Weston. He'll be assisting with Leah's prognosis."

"I read your first book," she said, and offered her hand.

"Only the first?" I grinned as I shook it.

"And I thought you only read Cosmo and romance novels." Kathleen looked at Leah's log. "No changes?" She hung the clipboard back on the bed.

"No, Dr. Scott. Just a very minor drop in her pulse about ninety minutes ago."

Like an angel on life-support, Leah was helpless.

Her black hair outlined her olive skin, and her face was without expression. Passive. Innocent. The tubes and sensors around her were like chains binding her to a physical presence that no longer mattered. She was away.

"She's definitely dreaming," I stated, watching her eyes move rhythmically under their lids.

"Yes," Rebecca confirmed, "she seems to go through regular cycles of REM, but…"

"But?" Kathleen prodded.

"Well, sometimes she stays in REM my entire shift."

They both turned as if I would have some profound analysis or insightful comment, but I didn't.

"Her mind's active. That much we know," I said, adding, "but she's elsewhere."

Kathleen made every effort to make Leah as comfortable as possible. After repositioning her sensors, she fluffed her pillows, then led me back into the hallway, continuing the tour.

"Tomorrow I'll introduce you to Dr. Young, the Chief Administrator. He wants to meet with you right away. Oh, and remember to wear a tie, he's kind of old school sometimes."

"Sounds like an interview."

"Well, a few rules have to be followed here. I spoke with him before calling you. I'm sure he just wants to see for himself that you're a competent professional—wants to meet you. You'd do the same thing."

"Hey, I'm in and out of here in a few days. I'll give you my best, then I'm back in LA this weekend."

"Typical," she smirked.

"What's that mean?"

"Nothing. All I'm saying is you can't contribute to a medical evaluation without certain protocol."

"Medical evaluation?" We both knew better. She wouldn't have called me if the case wasn't beyond medical boundaries.

"Look, I really don't know if I can be of any help, but I'd like to do some tests."

"I figured as much," she said. "Just don't start off like John Wayne coming to save the day," she added, concerned about my disposition.

"Well pilgrim," I grinned.

"No. I'm serious. I work here. I have to work with these people, and Dr. Young already thinks I'm crazy for entertaining the prospect of..."

"Of thought conveyance?" The term was used several times in my recent book, which I knew she'd read.

"No, not specifically." She grouped it all together. "The entire existence of sixth sense."

"Sounds a little narrow minded for a person in his position. And what if good ole Dr. Young doesn't like me?"

"I wouldn't worry about it. I mean, I'm sure you'll do just fine. But more importantly, why haven't you mentioned my hair?"

Because I preferred it longer. "It'll take some getting used to," I answered.

It had been a long day, but we finally ended up back on the fourth floor, where we hugged and said goodnight.

After reminding me to set my clock, wear a tie, and meet her in the main lobby the next morning, she continued down the hall.

———

Six o'clock came soon, but after a brisk shower, I tied my tie, straightened my jacket collar, and with a glance in the mirror ran my fingers through my hair. I was ready to meet Dr. Young.

The staff had grown considerably, and the intensity of the third floor the previous night had spread throughout the hospital.

Kathleen greeted me in the main lobby. "Before anything else, we need to get your ID."

She led directly to the Security Office.

"Morning, Greg. This is David Weston. He'll need a badge and key."

"Good morning, Dr. Scott," the Chief of Security said, then stood to greet me. "Nice to meet you Mr. Weston."

We shook hands, then he had me stand in front of a wall facing a camera, where he snapped a shot, entered some things on his keypad, and moments later handed me a laminated badge.

"Great, even worse than my driver's license."

"What security level, Dr. Scott?"

"Level five," she answered as she smiled at my unflattering photo.

"Five?" He looked curiously at Kathleen.

"Yes, five," she confirmed, turning assuredly to him and then me.

Shuffling through a filing cabinet, he handed me a questionnaire that took several minutes to complete.

He then entered my information into his computer and gave me a sensor key, like Kathleen's. "Keep this around your neck, and if you happen to lose it, call me immediately." He handed me his card. "This is my number, twenty-four hours a day, seven days a week, three-hundred and... "

"Three-hundred and sixty-five days a year," I interrupted. "I just won't lose it. How's that?"

We thanked him, shook hands again, and Kathleen led down the main floor hallway to Dr. Young's office.

A receptionist greeted us, then pressed the intercom. "Doctors Scott and Weston are here, Sir."

"Yes, yes, please show them in," an elderly voice responded.

When we stepped inside, it was immediately apparent that Dr. Young was an avid golfer, as he was putting at a custom green on the far side of his massive office. Three windows overlooked the scenery for which Meadowsview was named, and built-in mahogany bookshelves—with a collection that would put many libraries to shame—gave the room a sense of power and entitlement. It was clear that from this office came ultimate decisions, both medical and administrative. And the distinguished gray-haired man with the golf club made those decisions.

The desk and furniture was handcrafted, and on the far left wall were dozens of plaques and awards—tributes to his accomplishments. Arranged in circles like a large bulls-eye, the very center of the adornment was vacant, as though being reserved for one very special triumph.

He stood for a moment like he was at the Masters, then tapped the ball, and we all watched it drop into the hole. I considered throwing my hands in the air and shouting, 'And he scores!', but chose instead to exercise a degree of decorum.

"David, welcome to Meadowsview. I hope your room's accommodating."

"Yes. Thank you. The room's great."

"Dr. Scott has spoken very highly of you. Do you mind if I call you David?"

"No, not at all."

"Please, have a seat." He pulled one of the two chairs out for Kathleen.

In his mid-sixties, he was wearing canary yellow pants with a white golf shirt, and was plainly planning to play a round that morning.

My first impression was mixed. On one hand, he seemed pleasant, even jovial. But on the other, he came across as clever, a sophisticated man who was focused on the business side of the hospital.

Certainly, his position was demanding, but along with it came many perks, including leisurely afternoons on the links with other members of the board. Still, his standing was unquestionable. Dr. Young—The King of

Meadowsview—was in charge.

He reached into his desk and pulled out a folder marked with my name. Placing it on the desk in front of him, he reached into the drawer again and removed a copy of my third book.

"David, your writing's impressive, and your theories are... interesting." His tone was borderline patronizing, but I held my tongue. How could I be insulted by the opinion of someone I pictured in tacky pants on the back nine? Still, I couldn't help but glance at Kathleen, who appeared equally surprised by his tone.

"Dr. Scott requested your input on the Goforth children, and as a professional courtesy, I've consented." He added, again with the condescending tone, "But there will be certain stipulations and limits."

"What limits, specifically?" I asked.

"Dr. Scott, you're needed on the third floor please," the intercom interrupted before he could answer.

"Okay then." With a look telling me to keep my cool, "I'll meet up with you later," she said as she left the room.

Seeming to welcome her absence, Dr. Young began to define my inclusion on what I came to call The Goforth Situation.

"Okay David, I'll speak candidly. While I've had only limited involvement in this case, I respect Dr. Scott's opinions, and she's an invaluable member of our staff." He scratched his forehead. "However, as reluctant as I am to use this approach—and let's face it, your practice is quite unusual—our head of psychology has also expressed a degree of interest." Smiling, he picked up my book. "It seems you have a bit of a fan-base here at Meadowsview."

"All I know is a good friend asked me to come... I can autograph that if you want?" Grinning, I couldn't resist the dig.

"Well, thanks, but that's not necessary." He placed it back on the desk, and put his hands behind his head.

I almost laughed out loud, but managed to keep a straight face.

"But I *will* need a signature on your entry paperwork. The package includes Meadowsview policies and procedures, confidentiality agreements, the usual. Oh, but have you ever actually worked in this kind of environment?"

The conversation continued much the same for several minutes, as he made his position clear. Finally he alluded to my work. "How invasive are your procedures?"

"Minimally," I answered. "She's already asleep, so there's no need for any kind of sedation. But the sensors function better if they're attached directly to the scalp, so we'll need to shave her head."

"We?" he said. "I'm not much of a barber, so knock yourself out. Or, I suppose I could get a nurse to do that." He finished, "It's all up to you." With a quick smirk, he let it be known that he could either help or hinder my efforts.

Seeing that, while he was controlling, Dr. Young at least had a sense of humor, I smiled. "I'd certainly appreciate that."

"Well, what exactly do you do?"

The question was broad enough for interpretation, so I

attempted to impress him with technology. "I record specific chemical and electrical changes, and then use digital formulas to determine potential thought likeliness."

"Potential likeliness?" He smirked. "You mean 'possible' discoveries?" He enjoyed having the upper hand, it showed in his sardonic tone and physical posture.

"I mean likely to find something more than what's been discovered up to now." Not wanting to be too offensive, I added, "Respectfully."

We both sat back in our chairs, quietly squaring off as though in a staring contest, until he finally replied. "*You can't know what goes on in her head anymore than I can.*"

"I think that remains to be seen."

"So you tap regions of her brain and then what, a computer tells you what she thinks?"

"Not exactly, but it narrows it down quite a bit."

"And how do you verify the results?"

"When the subjects wake up they tell me what they dreamed of—objects, colors, sounds, other people…"

"I somehow doubt this patient will be waking up to confirm your test results," he said. But having consented to my presence, he hesitantly gave the green light for my procedures. "Everything will need to be coordinated with Dr. Feldman."

I nodded in agreement, glad that I would report to someone other than his royal majesty.

Ultimately, we enjoyed a laugh or two at each other's expense. His points were well taken, and I—more for Kathleen than myself—avoided being too derisive.

Moments later, he showed me to the door, where we politely shook hands, and he returned to his club and balls.

"Dr. Weston, if I could just get your signature on a few papers." The secretary stood and walked toward me with a folder. "There are a total of six places." She opened it and pointed to a line highlighted with a yellow marker. "Just look for the highlights, count to six and you're all set."

After meeting Dr. Young, and viewing several pages of legal jargon, I needed fresh air, so I decided to check out the grounds. Loosening my tie, I went directly to the front lobby, where the guard stood, not recognizing me, but quick to notice the administrative pass.

"I'm David Weston." I extended my hand. "I'll be in and out for a few days."

Following a footpath to the left side of the building, I headed northwest, nodding appreciatively at the gardeners, busy trimming the colorful landscaping in front of the building.

Within moments I was away from Meadowsview, inhaling the fresh air and trying not to think about the many things on my mind, especially my cravings for rum.

The path curved to the north, where the janitor I'd seen in the cafeteria the night before was sitting on a fallen tree trunk. Grinning, he almost seemed to be expecting me.

"I'm Kris," he said, and held out his hand.

"David," I responded with a final step toward him.

"So, mon, what brings you to Meadowview, huh? Is it da girl?" His Jamaican accent was strong. "She dreams," he flatly stated. "All da time, she dreams of da bridges."

"So, you've talked with Dr. Scott?"

"No. She doesn't talk to me. I'm just da floor guy. But she knows da girl dreams."

"But if she does dream, how do *you* know?"

"Kris knows many things, sees things. Her eyes flutter at night, and her brother... he knows her dreams. She dreams, he draws." With a self-assured smile, he seemed convinced that the twins were connected, gaining my full attention. What Kathleen had speculated was confirmed by, of all people, a member of the maintenance department. But his position didn't matter to me, it was the look in his eyes that sent the familiar rush through my veins.

"Ah, but what do I know? I'm just a janitor." Unexpectedly, he stood and began walking further away from the hospital. With a look over his shoulder, "Coming?" he asked.

I hadn't planned on company, but followed him for several minutes, curious about what was on his mind. Neither of us spoke until we came to a gravel road, where he turned as if he knew that something important was just ahead.

"If the trees spoke, I wonder what they would say?" Even in his small-talk there was a measure of mysticism.

"I don't know, but maybe they'd remind me to bring coffee and a doughnut next time."

"It's not very far now. Just past the next bend."

"What? What's up there?"

"You'll see," he answered, not wanting to say anything that might spoil his surprise.

A short distance ahead, the road curved and revealed an old covered bridge. About sixty feet across and ten feet wide, it spanned a ravine and narrow brook.

"Many bridges in this area. So many indeed. This one is over seventy years old. Many have crossed. So many lives, dreams trying to get to da other side. And da girl, she's trying to cross bridges here." He pointed to his forehead. "Ah, but she has troubles, many troubles. Someone tries to keep her from crossing."

"Who? Who keeps her from crossing?" As extreme as it all seemed, his analogy was compelling.

"You want me to do all da work for you? Look at da little one's drawings. He knows. Stay. Stay and check it out. This bridge. I wonder who made it?" He then headed back to the hospital, leaving me wondering how much credence I should grant him and this unusual outing.

The bridge was a simple design, but masterfully crafted. It had endured time and the elements quite well. Built entirely of wood, it had, as all bridges do, a unique character of its own, a sense of identity and purpose. As I began across, I heard Kris in the distance repeat, "I wonder who made it?"

Less than two days after considering the unthinkable, I stood on the bridge, diverting my attention from the numbing memories that had turned my life into a contradiction of want and will. Away from the brick building where I felt as if everyone saw through my charade of confidence, I found comfort in the peaceful setting. Dragging my fingers over the wooden slats, I inspected the crossing closely, and in the middle, the initials "JMG 1940" were etched into a supporting beam.

Leah felt small as she looked at the mountains before her. Scurrying across the frozen tundra, her stare was fixed on the statuesque peaks ahead. *What's up there?* With no intention of going back, she avoided turning to the black steed behind her.

She knew that it was getting closer, but this was *her* dream. Surely, if she ignored its presence, it would cease to exist.

She wanted only to separate the past from the present, and nothing could change her mind, not even Elijah.

It's not fair, she thought. But few things were fair in Leah's life, and here, in the fragile recesses of her imagination, she tried to keep from thinking of her twin. *Don't think about him... think about what might be up there in those mountains!*

"But it's not fair," she said out loud, to which the horse responded with angry snorts.

Looking behind her, she saw that it was closer than she thought.

Determined to take a look at the Goforth files, I headed back to Meadowsview, where I was greeted by the receptionist. "Doctor Weston, Doctor Scott left a message for you to meet her in the Imaging Lab."

"Okay, but where is it?"

"Third floor, down the hall, through the double doors, and on the right," she answered in a mundane tone, with a pasted-on smile, one that surely comes from facing the same window and answering the same questions day after day for many years.

"Third floor, down the hall, through the double doors," I repeated, returning the smile as I adjusted my jacket and tie.

The room was dark—the windows completely blocked with various sized light boxes.

Kathleen stood viewing images on a large screen and a doctor was looking closely at a transparency on the far side of the room.

"David, this is Dr. Jon Svelgaard, a neurosurgeon. Jon monitors our coma patients, among other things."

"Yes, yes… my many hats," he grinned, and with only a glance and slight wave, he turned back to the film. "There's a possible increase in pressure, but this," he pointed to a small oval on the x-ray. "This is unusual."

"What is it?" she asked and took several steps in his direction. She leaned closer to the box. "Was this spot here before, Jon? I don't remember seeing it."

"About the size of the tip of a pencil." He placed a finger on his chin. "Located in the lateral pons."

With a gaze at Kathleen, I moved closer, viewing the mark positioned squarely in a part of the brainstem where dreams commence.

"We do need to place a bolt." He faced Kathleen, who was suddenly silent and didn't respond. She went to a desk, where she wrote notes until he followed.

"It's not an optional procedure," he flatly stated. "And you're aware of that."

Trying to at least appear to be minding my own business, I looked around the room, surprised by his reprimanding tone.

"We've worked together for awhile now, and I know you're aware that this is standard practice."

"Look, I'm the one who determines Miss Goforth's procedures, not you, doctor. So why do we have to keep going over this?"

"Are you really going to put me in the position of having to...?"

"Having to what, Jon, go over my head? Go ahead. It's still *my* call."

"Well, you're calling it wrong... and of course this has nothing to do with..."

"David, I think we're done here," she interrupted with a bitter stare at the neurosurgeon.

"What was that all about?" I asked as the door closed behind us.

"Nothing," she answered flatly. "Nothing I can't handle."

Her demeanor was different as Kathleen led me to Leah's room. Her exchange with Dr. Svelgaard had hit a nerve.

Viewing the log, she recorded more notes as I looked at Leah, a beautiful child, with long black hair, olive skin, and high cheekbones. It seemed obvious that she was at least part Indian.

"Native American?" I asked.

"Well, yes. Her mother's full-blooded Cherokee."

Her arms were folded across her waist, and Leah appeared to be peacefully sleeping, even with electrodes attached to her head, chest, fingers, and toes.

After giving the nurse instructions, "Ready?" Kathleen asked, and led me to the elevators. "So, did you look at the files?" She knew I hadn't.

"No, I needed a walk after meeting the good Doctor Young."

"It went that well, huh? Hey, I think I have a few minutes. Are you hungry?"

"Starved."

She had just put her tray on the metal rails when a page came over the public address system. "Dr. Scott, come to the third floor, please."

"Duty calls," she said, and snatched a roll from a basket at the end of the buffet. "Tell you what, you stay and have lunch. We'll talk at dinner. I have a couple of other patients to see. And David, do take a look at those files." Taking a bite, she turned away, surely still thinking about her row with Jon.

"Meatloaf or pasta?" The server asked.

"How's the meatloaf?" I responded, turning to Kathleen, who hesitated before disappearing into the hallway.

"Glad to see you didn't get lost, mon."

"I was a Boy Scout, mon." Returning the sarcasm, I was surprised when Kris sat across the table and began ravenously devouring his lunch.

"Did you find something?" he asked with a mouthful.

"JMG—who is he?"

After swallowing his bite, he answered, "I guess dat be the one who made it, eh?" Grinning like a Cheshire cat, he chugged his iced tea. He was just trying to be funny, so I let it ride, but he continued. "Aren't *you* supposed to be da expert here?"

I leaned slightly across the table and responded in a lower tone. "Look, as witty as you are, I don't have time for twenty questions with the local humorist." Of course, he was funny, likable, and seemed to have some kind of inside track with the twins. But despite his apparent talents, he gave the impression of merely dangling a carrot—I needed to know, and if there was really anything he could offer, he needed to tell me.

Surprised by my bluntness, he swallowed another mouthful and sat straight up. "Okay. In town is a library. Many records, much history..." His change of manner revealed a side of him I'd not yet seen, gaining not only my curiosity, but also a degree of admiration. "And JMG is for Joseph Michael Goforth."

"What?" Surprised, my chin dropped and I stared for a moment, questioning the statement.

"Yes, Goforth," he answered, adding, "a very wealthy man."

"And this is from a book? What book? Can you show me, or do you have to go back to work?"

"No work today, only nights, and da book is in my room." He finished his lunch and sat staring at me. "Mon, you eat slow."

"I like to actually taste my food."

45

"Dat bridge, the one you were on, is called Goforth's Crossing," he said. "And as far as da eye can see... east, west, north and south, he owns it all. *All* of it!" Amazed that one man could have such wealth, he shook his head in disbelief.

"Joseph? The bridge? What else do you know?"

"It's all right there in black and white."

Chapter 3 – Leah

"Our rooms are on four," Kris said when I pressed the button for the third floor. "Or have you forgotten?"

"No, I haven't forgotten. But I need to get something first."

"Do as you will. I'm in 405."

I swiped my key, the door buzzed, and I went directly to the cabinet drawer labeled 'Go – Gz'. *Gocek, Godfrey.* I thumbed through the files. *Goforth.* Inside the sleeve were two thick envelopes, one for Elijah, and the other, Leah.

Taking only Leah's file, I initialed a clipboard hanging on the cabinet and, with a sense of now being officially involved in the Goforth case, I left the room. The door closed behind me and I walked down the hallway, holding an envelope containing pages I hoped would provide me with insight and direction.

I placed my shoes near the door, sat on the bed and picked up my recorder. *What brought this girl here?* With two pillows propped against the large headboard, I leaned back and began reading.

Labeled, 'Leah Anne Goforth - LAG270301', the pages in her file were easily over two inches thick, and all entries were chronological, the most recent on top. Wanting to start at the beginning, I turned the entire stack over and placed it on the bed to my left.

Like a 'How to' on ways to abuse a child, the pages were disturbing. "Hypothenar eminence, occipital scalp, sacral area..." The terms were serious, and it was apparent that her injuries weren't merely bumps and bruises. After noting several trips to the emergency room, I stopped counting, unsurprised that following each visit she was again released to her parents.

Other than entries by Dr. Svelgaard, the file was a pre-Meadowsview assemblage of Leah's medical history. Discouraging, the pages were also a statement of her resilience. What kind of monster could inflict such pain? She had endured so much in her short life—was it any wonder that she finally just shut down?

"Leah Goforth," I said into a small tape recorder. Viewing the pages, I remembered Kathleen saying her mother was Indian. "Twelve years old, mother's Cherokee, subject of physical and emotional abuse." I sat with a growing sense of compassion and sympathy for the twins.

The causes of Leah's visits to the ER were always stated as accidental, except for one logged by a staff psychologist, Dr. Lambert, who notified the Huntington

Police Department. After that, she and Elijah became wards of the state of West Virginia.

This was her tragic story, and now Leah lay unconscious in a room across the hall from her brother, who was surrounded by uncertainty. It was beyond disheartening, beyond sad, and beyond explanation.

Feeling ashamed about my own recent contemplations, I turned the pages seeking reasons and answers. *Answers?* What answers could there be? And what reasons could justify, or pardon, the actions leading to the surrender of a child whose only worry should've been tomorrow's math test?

The pages at my fingertips were a written testimony of life's undue pain and cruelty, causing me to briefly count my own blessings, and Kathleen was one of them. I thought of her scent, how light reflected on her hair, the sound of her laughter, and pensive look which was always followed by her twisting her hair. She was the reason I was at Meadowsview, and yet I had no clear reason for having refused her calls. There was nothing I could say, no magic phrase that could explain the impact of my private torment.

— — —

Leah existed only subliminally, her frail body merely hosting the complexities of her dream.

Shivering under layers of ragged clothes, she trudged on, knowing that darkness would be even more relentless, and praying that the mountains would lead to sanctuary.

With her arms drawn tightly across her chest, she

fought the blistering wind-chill, feeling like a small figure in a wintry snow globe, unable to break free. Trying to sustain the listless pace, she grit her teeth as she faced the west.

The black stallion followed, and Leah knew that the menacing steed was even closer now. She tried to ignore it, and not look behind her, but the sound of its hoofs and persistent neighs grew louder, more threatening.

Finally she could take no more. Stopping, she faced it again.

Like an ebony statue, the horse stood still. For several moments—seeming much longer to Leah—they stared intensely into each other's eyes. The only movement was their cold breaths, exhaled into the wind, which swept them away.

Wanting to appear strong, Leah knew that any sign of weakness would be sensed by the figure which stood only twenty or so paces away. If she flinched, dire consequences could follow, and she dare not turn away.

Lifting a front leg, the horse drug a hoof on the frozen earth, and began to bob its head from side to side, a sign that it was about to charge.

"Run, Leah..." a girl's voice was at first only a whisper. "Run!" she repeated, "Run to the valley!"

Leah turned behind her, to the icy cliffs, and at this the stallion stood on its hind legs, preparing to attack.

Chased by the dark creature that had found its way into her dream, she ran. Coming to the cliffs, she noticed a narrow passage. *There, s*he thought. *I can make it!*

The sprinting horse was almost upon her when she entered the crevice. Her heart pounding, she ran several steps further before turning to the angry eyes of the beast, which was unable to fit into the corridor where its prey stood weeping.

Hoping to find clues to the puzzle, I continued to read Leah's file, but only found more despair. The tragic chronicles of Leah Anne Goforth—from the earliest, *fell off swingset*, to the more recent, *abdominal bleeding*—weren't easy to read. Then I came to a page on which several lines had been highlighted with a fluorescent marker.

Cognitive of her surroundings and situation; extremely intelligent, articulate, and well-mannered. Spoke of her father's anger over her ability to "Tell what's going to happen before it happens."
During our session she said, "The napkins are in your top drawer," seconds before I spilled coffee. She also handed me my cell phone just before it rang.
Possibly precognitive.

Encouraged, I started looking for more pages written by Dr. Lambert, but was startled by a knock on the door.

"Planning to skip dinner altogether or what?" Kathleen asked.

"I guess I kind of lost track of time," I answered, then bluntly asked, "How much of her file have you read?"

"Well, most, but not all of it." She looked embarrassed as she stepped inside. "I read about half of it, then got sidetracked."

"Did you start at the beginning, or with the most recent pages?"

"I started at the top of the file. Why?" Without giving me a chance to answer, she added, "When they were first admitted I read what I could. Okay?"

Having always known her to be more thorough, I couldn't help thinking that I'd had greater input from the janitor than from Kathleen.

"So, coming to dinner or what?"

Although I was hungry, I wasn't in the best frame of mind. "No. I think I'll do a little more reading..."

"Oh, so now you're gonna punish me?"

"What? No one's punishing you."

"So typical. Ya know, it's not like this is *all* I'm dealing with. I do have other patients, and each one of them needs constant evaluation, medication changes, this test, that test..."

"I just thought you'd read the file, that's all."

"Well *excuse me*." With a stanch southern twang, she went on, "I'm just a simple ole country girl."

"I didn't mean it that way, so don't even go there."

"Well, let's see, you've only been here two days, and are giving me a performance evaluation? Unbelievable," she frowned. "And this from a guy who can't be bothered to either answer or return calls."

"Look, I'm sorry. I didn't mean to piss you off."

"Pissed off? You think *this* is pissed off? No David, 'pissed off' was a while ago, when I hadn't heard from you in almost a year, and had to hear from your brother that you'd been ignoring pretty much everything but your work and drinking." She lowered her tone and continued.

"Look, I don't know why you cut off contact, maybe I really don't even want to know, but we need to work together on this. I mean, I need your help, not your critique." Pausing, she drew a deep breath as I put an arm around her. She then pounded my chest with one fist. "And you, David Weston, are coming to dinner with me. I'm starving."

That about settled it. I slipped into my shoes and made a mental note to try to be more sensitive.

Our walk down the hallway was lonely, both of us feeling a degree of inadequacy, but in the elevator she stared at the floor, then placed her hand in mine.

"I'm sorry," I said, facing her. "I didn't mean to sound judgmental."

"And I really meant to read the whole file, but it's so depressing."

"Perplexing," I responded with a grin.

"Discouraging," she said.

"Intriguing."

As we stepped through the metal doorway, she shook her head. "Heartbreaking."

"Amazing," I mumbled, smiling at the banter which had become a benchmark of our relationship.

During dinner she talked about her other patients, illustrating the range of her responsibilities. Her dedication wasn't surprising, nor were the sad stories, and seemingly hopeless condition of several of those under her care.

"We have a guy who was struck by lightning, and may never talk again. And a thirty-two-year-old mother, a hit and run victim. She's been unconscious for five weeks now. Even if she comes out of it she probably won't know her own name."

And all I knew was the Goforth children. One case.

"I've discussed you with Dr. Feldman, the head of psychiatry. Apparently she's a fan," she smirked. "Anyway, you'll meet her tomorrow morning. Listen, I didn't bring you from Los Angeles to have you sit on the sidelines. Be assertive, but remember, everything you do needs her approval."

"No problem." I nodded.

"In advance," she said firmly. "Just remember, no John Wayne stuff. This isn't True Grit, and you aren't the Duke."

"No Rooster Cogburn?" I answered, feigning disappointment. "Maybe we'll get lucky," I said. "But I'll need a lot of help."

"Of course, I'll help in every way."

I felt worse about my seclusion. There she was, mired in other problems, but moving forward, taking logical steps. She knew that doctors and medicine, even those at Meadowsview, could only do so much in their attempts to awaken someone from a dream. That was where I came in.

Of course, outwardly, I came across as self-assured and confident. But in truth, wherever I was, whatever I was doing, I felt like I should be somewhere else, doing something completely different.

— — —

With ice seeping through the holes in her shoes, Leah's toes were numb.

What's this? Could it be? Footprints had been left in the snow. Then, for only an instant, the icy glare was gone, and she saw a spec on the horizon.

Let this be someone who can help me. She closed her eyes, appealing to a greater glory.

"Faster Leah, faster," the words were at first faint, and then, like before, louder. "Come on!"

Dwarfed between the huge crags, and fighting unbearable fatigue, Leah tried to gather her strength, but with every step the wind was more ruthless. The clouds thickened and the sky became darker as she tried desperately to call out. "Wait... wait..." but in the cold air, her strength drained, she could only whisper the words. Having lost sight of the traveler ahead, she tried once more, and this time the word echoed through the valley. "Wait..."

On elastic legs, she managed to take only a few more steps before collapsing on the frozen earth, where her body was layered in sheets of drifting snow. Unable to regain her footing, she lay shivering, trying to hold back the tears that turned to ice on her cheeks. She'd known this feeling too many times before.

Taking shallow, infrequent breaths, she was close to surrender when she heard a man's voice.

Faint, muffled, "I'm coming..." he said. "I'm coming..." Then he was there. Kneeling, he brushed the snow from her brow. "You're safe now," he assured. "You're okay." He draped her body over his shoulder and turned to the faintly lit western sky. "Girl, someone up there likes you."

When we were finished eating, Kris approached and placed a book on my side of the table.

"Dis is it, mon," he said as Kathleen watched curiously. "And I marked some pages for you."

I thanked him and he left with his usual strut and smile as he passed the servers.

"What's that?" she asked, looking first at the book and then at me.

I recognized her disapproving expression, and, having heard directly from him that they weren't exactly friends, I tried to understate it. "It's just a book he was telling me about." I hoped that would be enough to humor her, but it wasn't.

"What *kind* of book?" She reached across the table and slid it toward her. "Early Twentieth Century Families of Vermont?" She flipped through the pages, until coming to the first one Kris had bookmarked. Raising her eyebrows, "Goforth?" she asked, then turned to the next page, one that detailed the Goforth family tree.

I watched without comment, wondering what we'd find inside.

Flipping to the last bookmarked page, Kathleen's face went flush.

It was an old sepia photograph of a young man standing under the awning of the bridge I'd crossed that morning.

"David, this bridge was in my dream. What's going on?" She placed the opened hardback on the table to her right and glared at the image.

"When was the last time you were there?" I asked, thinking that she'd merely projected it into her dream.

"What? I've never been there."

Surprised, I pointed northwest. "So it's only about a mile from here, but you've never been there?"

"No, never seen it before now and..."

"Then how do you know it's the same one?"

"I *know* it is," she answered.

"A lot of those old bridges look alike, so how can you be..."

"Look, I'm sure... See the arch here?" She pointed to the entry, and the same distinctive Gothic arch that had caught my attention that morning. "It's the same bridge."

At a loss, she continued. "I've heard of a covered bridge nearby, but just never really thought about it."

"I'm surprised you never shot photos. But maybe you've seen pictures, postcards?"

"No. I'm pretty sure I'd never seen it before the dream. But what difference does it make? I mean, even if I'd seen it before, how could Elijah have known what I dreamt?" She twisted her hair. "It doesn't make sense."

"Primordial instinct. Telepathy." To me it *did* make sense. "He received your thought waves."

Occurrences like this were the backbone of my construct on Waves of Transitional Fractals—WTF.

Combining elements of Chaos Math and the Collective Unconscious, my theory drew heavily from the writings of Carl Jung and Edward Lorenz.

To my friends, I called it the 'What the Fuck' theory, and phrased it in humorous terms—especially after I'd had a few drinks. And they were, of course, more than happy to give their own critiques and conjectures.

Synchronicity. The Butterfly Effect. The latter seemed to draw the most laughs, and Kathleen even threw an occasional jab.

"So a butterfly flaps its wings in Central Park, and a tornado hits Tulsa. Right?"

I took it in stride, laughed along, and even gave my own one-liners now and then.

The official statement was unsupported, presenting a field day for my colleagues.

"Fractals of displaced energy cross the time and space continuum. In REM states of unconsciousness, perceptions are heightened, resulting in greater incidents of thought conveyance."

Scrutinized, picked apart by my most vocal detractors, WTF was at first outright rejected, and rightfully so. Something was missing. But when I returned from Lauani, the full thesis developed...

Contriving a demonstration—one that would give credence to the possibility of dream-sharing—I sent e-mails and posted invitations on several campus bulletin boards.

"Do telepathic dream states occur?" The title was intended to weed out those with no interest in paranormal psychology, but ambiguous enough to draw a moderate crowd.

The evening of the lecture, I stood in my closet and, after trying on several ties, chose a black one that matched my jacket and shirt. What if nobody showed up?

The gravity of this night couldn't be underestimated. If I failed to gain an audience, or at the very least, present a solid basis for WTF, my studies would become meaningless.

The drive from my home to Westwood was nerve racking. I drew deep breaths and tried to think about the presentation, but also prepared myself for the possibility that the room would be empty.

"Good. You're here early." I was greeted by Gerard Dubois, head of the department. Until then he'd shown only mild interest in my work, but in an uncharacteristic tone, his voice held a measure of excitement. "We've had to move you from the lecture hall to a larger venue."

My face went flush. I'd thought of nothing but the possibility of being shunned, dismissed by those who could make or break me. Now I was to address a much larger group than I'd expected—and had an entirely new set of reasons to be worried.

Gerard led me to the side entry of an auditorium. "Will you need any help?" he asked, pointing to the large piece of luggage I rolled behind me.

"Just a table. I think I have everything else."

I stepped through a wide doorway, onto the stage, and saw that there were already over two-hundred people seated. Others stood in the aisles, and the lobby was packed. Overwhelmed, I could see, forty-five minutes before I began, that I'd be addressing a standing room only audience. Drawing deep breaths, I was relieved when John arrived.

"Bro, you're a rock star! Have you seen how many people are here?" He walked past me, straight to the stage. Right at home being the center of attention, John waved to the crowd.

I couldn't help but smile. Confident, he almost came across as arrogant or unaffected. But his sense of humor and charisma were infectious.

"By the way," he said backstage, "I smoked a joint on the way here."

"Great. That's just great." I shook my head. "Did you remember the presentation?"

"Yes, of course," he responded. "Wait. I forgot the laptop." He kept a straight face. "Just kidding," he finally said. "But damn, you shoulda seen your expression..."

"Not now, okay? A lot's riding on this." This was it. I was hoping for forty or fifty, but the hall was filled with over four-hundred people.

"Lighten up. I know you're nervous, but everything will work out. You'll do fine."

"I'm not worried about *me*. I was just hoping that maybe you'd show up straight for a change."

"Don't be a bitch," he responded. "I'll run the graphics, you give the presentation—just like we practiced. It's only a *slightly* larger crowd than you expected." He laughed, then took a different tone. "Seriously. You know this backwards and sideways. And this is *your* night—*own* it."

And he was absolutely right. I knew every word of my mandate. I was prepared. But among the faces in the front row—like vultures, waiting to pick the remnants from a carcass—were several of my colleagues. Most of them there only to watch me fall flat on my face, and while we powered the computers, they exchanged cordial greetings with one another.

"This is it," I said. "I guess I can always teach..."

"Maybe this isn't the best time to second guess yourself? You know what to do and how to do it." Like a coach giving a pep-talk, he put a hand on my shoulder. "Stay focused. This is your shot. This is your time to shine. So *shine*. You can do this."

We finished setting up the presentation with only minutes to spare before showtime. John sat beside a table that held two laptops, and five wireless headsets.

I approached the podium, my hands hidden in the pockets of my coat. As I adjusted the height of the mic, I tried to hide the fact that I was petrified.

Any hesitation would be seen as self-doubt—the last thing I wanted to convey—so I began right away.

"Okay," I said. "I think we're ready to get started. First, I'd like to thank each of you for coming. Clearly, we weren't expecting this big an audience." I turned to Gerard, who dimmed the lights. Then I faced John, who pressed a single key on the laptop, starting the presentation.

The title, "Waves of Transitional Fractals," appeared on the large monitor behind me, then a combination of photographs and video clips flashed on the screen. Surreal, thought provoking, the graphics were a way of getting their attention.

"If I could have a few volunteers," I said, to which several hands raised.

I picked up four headsets, walked down the main aisle, and handed them out. Returning to the stage, I put the last set on, and began speaking through the mic, to those with the other headsets.

"Thank you for volunteering," I said. "Each of you will hear words. All you have to do is count to three, then say the word into your mic."

I addressed the audience. "Think of your mind as a two-way radio—a receiver and sender of energy."

A loud, crowded city street appeared on the monitor behind me.

"Normal perception occurs during conscious states. Our surroundings, sounds, smells, tastes, interactions. What affects our daily lives triggers conscious reactions."

The scene changed, replaced by a painting by Salvador Dali, *The Persistence of Memory.* A clock melting.

"Subconscious perception happens in dream states, during REM sleep."

John pressed a series of commands, and each volunteer began hearing a unique set of words.

"Bluebird."

"Confetti."

"Zebra."

As instructed, they repeated the reference words, triggering images that briefly flashed on the screen.

Then John shifted gears—the words and images came faster.

"Feathers."

"Trapeze."

"Lion."

"Octagon."

"Wave fractals travel across an infinite number of paths," I said. "In unconscious states, chemical changes allow our minds to receive and transmit over different routes—alternate frequencies." Of course, the premise was unproven, and the presentation, in some ways, was only smoke and mirrors.

John raised the speaker volume, put an echo on two of the mics, and a delay on the other two. He also distorted the images on the large screen—twisting, melting, fading. The result was an orchestrated display of dreamlike sights and sounds that brought the audience to the edge of their seats.

We continued until I abruptly gave the signal. Then, simultaneously, John ended the presentation, and Gerard turned on the lights.

"Then, we wake up," I said.

For several seconds, the auditorium was silent, leaving a pit in my stomach. I literally quit breathing for a moment, then turned to John.

Finally, someone began to clap, and the others joined in an impressive ovation. I could breathe again.

Staring through the window, Kathleen looked like a lost little girl. Though she tried to appear unaffected, her eyes were filled with confusion.

"So... thought devolution, huh? I knew this would be right up your alley." She tried to smile, but couldn't.

"He tuned in," I responded.

"I just don't get how that can happen. But if he's able to tune in to me..."

"You said she was in your dream. My guess is they were both there."

"What do you mean *there*? You mean I just dreamt about them, right?"

"No. I mean they were present, by proxy."

"Now you're just trying to confuse me," she said. "What do you mean by proxy? Put it in plain English."

"Imagine your thoughts as a single wave of light. Elijah's, and Leah's, as two other waves, running parallel to yours. Okay?"

"K," she said.

"Something causes one wave to change its course, and cross over the others. This creates the proxy—a new wave caused by the refraction of existing waves."

"I think I get it. But it's just so abstract—kinda like the whole butterfly thing."

"Not really," I said, then changed subjects. "So, how's the photography? Still take pictures?"

"Sometimes. Not nearly as much as I used to. I just never seem to have much time."

"I'm surprised you haven't been to that bridge, Ansel." I grinned.

"Oh well," she said. "Guess I'll have to settle for being a doctor."

"Well, for what it's worth, he's got nothing on you. You have a gift." It was true. Kathleen had an uncommon way of seeing common things, and a natural understanding of light.

"You've always said that," she answered. "You even tried to talk me into becoming a photographer. I remember it well." She laughed. "Our freshman year. You said, and I quote, 'You should just give up on medicine—do your own thing.' Those were your exact words."

"It was a compliment—not a suggestion. Just my way of saying you take good photos. But maybe you should've stuck with it. I mean, you're married to your career." Devoted, driven, she never put less than her full effort into anything she did. And the reward for her dedication was a room on the fourth floor, where she was at Meadowsview's beckon call.

"I know," she answered. "Trust me. I feel like one of the fixtures around here."

"Why don't you get your own place?"

"I've looked at a few. Just haven't found the right one."

"Well. I guess when you're ready to have an actual *life*, you'll find a home. Know what I mean, Kate?"

"Yeah," she answered. "But *then* what? I buy a house, sprout roots here, and that's *it?* Do you ever feel like..."

"Like there's gotta be more?" I said. "Everyday."

We both sat quietly staring into the dark. Nothing more needed to be said. For being so different in many ways, we were very much alike in others.

I finally broke the silence. "I should probably do some reading."

"Don't go." Her eyes met mine in the glass.

Rebecca was engulfed in another magazine, and didn't notice, but Kris watched Leah breathing.

"It's okay, child," he whispered, clutching a cold hand, and noticing a light mist coming from her mouth.

With a glance at Kris and then Leah, "Oh my God!"

Rebecca said, and stood as the magazines fell to the floor. "Has she been like this for long?"

"Since you were reading the last one," he grinned.

"Well, you just keep that quiet." She pressed the intercom button. "Karen, there's a notable decline in Leah's pulse and temperature."

Kris discreetly left the room as the third shift Head Nurse entered. Looking at the monitor, "Reduced heartbeat and blood pressure," Karen said. She faced Rebecca. "How long has she been like this?"

"A few minutes now," the student answered. "Should we page Doctor Scott?"

Without reply, Karen checked Leah's sensors and IV.

Rebecca quickly picked up the magazines from the floor, avoiding eye contact with her superior.

The head nurse had little tolerance for negligence, and would deal with her later. With a stern look, she sat in the chair where Kris had been.

Steadily, Leah's vital signs returned to normal. Karen recorded the incident in the patient's log, and then turned to face Rebecca. "Meadowsview is a very prestigious assignment for *any* student." She placed her on notice. "I'd hate to recommend that you don't return next semester. If there's any change in her condition, I expect to be alerted immediately. You're not here to read fashion magazines. Are we on the same page?"

Embarrassed, Rebecca nodded, and Karen responded to another call.

———

In his room, across the hall from his sister, Elijah was

sketching, while Kris stood just inside the doorway.

This little boy should be sleeping, he thought.

Elijah didn't look up. "But I'm not sleepy," he responded, sounding almost robotic.

Where is she now?

"Close to the ice bridge," Elijah answered, raising his head with a blank stare. His arms, shoulders and wrists appeared strangely contorted as he continued to draw.

"And is that what you're drawing?" Kris asked aloud.

Elijah looked at Kris through the corners of his eyes, and after several seconds, he nodded.

— — —

Leah awakened on the shoulder of the familiar stranger, and raised her head to the faint glow of morning. Reaching toward the remnant clouds, the cliffs were now far away and resembled towering temples set against an amber sky.

"You're okay now," her rescuer said as he gently stood her on the snow covered ground.

Turning to him, she lifted the hood of his coat, revealing the face of a smiling black man, his dreadlocks partly dusted with snow.

Leah tried to keep up, taking two steps to each of his. She then took his hand, to which he looked down and smiled. "Oh girl, how did you get into this mess?"

"I'm dreaming," she answered without hesitation.

Lifting her again to his shoulders, he cupped her cold fingers, and from her new vantage point, daybreak revealed the desolate, ice-covered plain they traveled.

"I'm Leah. What's your name?"

"Kris," he replied. "And I'm very pleased to meet you, Leah."

"And I'm very pleased to meet you too," she said with a giggle.

"So why don't you just wake up?"

"Because I *can't* wake up, the journey's not over." She gripped his shoulders.

"But why am *I* here?"

"To help me get there!" She leaned back playfully.

"I'm here to help you get *where*?"

"There!" she replied, laughing and pointing ahead. "We're off to see the Wizard! I'm Dorothy, and you, you can be the Scarecrow!"

"Oh, so now I get to be some mindless guy made of straw?" He looked up as she leaned down smiling.

"Would you rather be the Tin Man, or maybe the Cowardly Lion?"

"Oh brothah," he said. "I suppose da Scarecrow will do." Playing the part, he shuffled his feet in the snow.

Near the top of a snowy ridge, she gasped, and clutched his shoulders tighter. "Kris!"

A few steps further he stopped and put her on her feet again. Directly ahead was a deep ravine, the two sides linked only by a crude, ice-covered bridge made of rope and wood.

Chapter 4 - First Crossing

Little more was said, as Kathleen remained in the solitude of uncertainty. The need to understand her dreams was written in her eyes, and I knew she wanted answers, but instead of offering a professional conjecture, I sat quietly.

She looked across the table and extended a hand, which I cupped with one of mine. "Well," leaning closer, she whispered, "at least I have you to help me understand this."

She'd always seemed like a pillar, able to withstand whatever life threw her way, but in the dim light of the cafeteria, Kathleen vulnerably gripped my hand tighter.

"Do you remember anything else?"

"No. Like what?"

"Anything... colors, sounds?"

She turned again to the window, and then back. "No, I

can only remember the bridge. Wait... No. I don't know. There was Leah and maybe something else." With her gaze fixed on the button of my shirt pocket, she shook her head and seemed quick to give up. "I don't know. I can't remember."

"Are you sure?"

"No. I mean yes, I'm sure," she responded.

"Maybe you should keep a log of your dreams."

"For what?"

"Well, there's no telling what you've forgotten. You could keep a tape recorder beside your bed, and when you wake up just turn it on. Talk about whatever you've dreamt."

"And?"

"And then give it to me each morning."

"Oh, you mean until this weekend?" The hold on my fingers was released. "And then what? Then I don't hear from you for another year, maybe two?"

Caught off guard, I responded, "Look, I'd prefer not to go into it right now."

"Of course you would," she said. "And if I hadn't called John every other week I wouldn't have known if you were dead or alive."

"What?"

"Hello? Wake up, David. I've had several talks with your brother."

"Is that right?"

"Yes, that's right," she mocked. "Just because you apparently couldn't care less how *I* was doesn't mean I stopped caring about you."

I didn't reply. She knew better.

"John sure seems to think you—how did he phrase it? 'Changed' when you got back from Indonesia."

"Polynesia."

"Whatever. *Polynesia*... The point is, I don't know, I mean, maybe I just feel like I should at least hear from *you* why you quit talking to me? I think you owe me that much."

"You know how John tends to elaborate."

"Right." Shaking her head, she looked away, her reflection now guarded, as if my hiatus had a deeper effect than I knew. "If something happened it's okay to tell me, ya know? I really hope you know you can come to me. I mean, come on, we've known each other a long time."

I wasn't ready to discuss Lauani, and to her noticeable frustration, remained quiet. Part of me really wanted to tell her the whole story, but despite the time that had passed, the wound was fresh. "Can we just do one thing at a time?"

"No. Yes. I mean, yes, of course. That's fine. It's cool. I just thought... well I guess it doesn't really matter what I thought, does it?"

"Try to remember your dream. Was it day or night?"

"Night," she answered with a stare that let me know she wasn't done with the previous subject, and after a short silence, she gave up. "I can't remember. Look, it's late, and I still need to look at some test results."

What does she want me to say? What would she think if I told her?

Emotionally spent, we went to the fourth floor, where we stood in front of my door.

"Night, Kate."

I turned to the pages of Leah's file, neatly stacked on one pillow, and after taking off my shirt, I fell thoughtlessly across the bed, causing several pages to plunge to the floor. Drawn to the scribbling on a page laying face down, I placed it beside me, then stacked the other pages and began to read. Typewritten, as were all of Dr. Lambert's reports, it was from a more recent session than the other one I'd read.

Despite our efforts, Leah has withdrawn into a post-trauma induced state of alpha-comatose; Complete emotional shutdown; Initial tests indicate atypical cerebral activity; Vital signs strong but patient unresponsive to attempted stimulus.

I flipped the page over, noting the scribbling that had caught my attention. The psychologist had written a single word, around which she had clearly spent awhile doodling in symmetrical lines, circles and triangles. The word was 'foresight'.

As I riffled through the pages I found an entry that both disturbed and thrilled me at once.

Due to Leah's condition, Elijah hasn't been told about their mother's death; He has become more isolated, and refuses to eat or sleep.

A cold chill ran through my neck when I realized that Leah's mother had died shortly *after* Leah had shut down.

I held the mic to my lips and began recording. "Dr. Lambert's reports indicate a strong possibility that Leah foresaw her mother's death." It made sense.

I placed the recorder on the nightstand, and lay staring at the ceiling. *What's missing? Damnit. Concentrate.* I tried to focus, but, like too many times before, my thoughts fell upon the white sand of Lauani...

Pure, the landscape and its inhabitants reflected a sense of primitive harmony—a village whose needs of shelter, food, and family didn't require a Mercedes or trips to Paris. There, happiness wasn't a measure of one's standing, but the standing of one's content.

Though cut short, my time with the islanders was riveting, and they were equally amazed by me. They watched every move, wide-eyed, and curious—as if I was a magician who performed tricks for their entertainment.

―――

I decided to check out the snacks in the cafeteria vending machines. In slacks, a tee-shirt and black sandals, I went to the elevator and pressed the button for the third floor. The doors had closed behind me when I realized that I was on the patient's floor.

I'll check on Leah.

At a room where three nurses responded to an elderly man's seizure, I watched until one came through the door with a curious look.

"Good morning," I said.

"Can I help you?" she asked with a glance at my feet.

"I'm just, uh," I looked down and smiled at my footwear. "I'm David Weston."

"Oh, yes," she replied.

"I got off on the wrong floor and thought I'd check on Leah Goforth."

"Of course," she smiled and pointed to the far end of the hallway.

As I approached her room I was surprised to see Kris holding Leah's hand. He read aloud from a sports magazine and commented as though she were merely sick, rather than in a deep coma. Unnoticed, I stood watching while he continued to read, complete with lively narrative. "See! I *knew* they would have a great year!"

Rebecca turned Leah to her other side, and jotted notes in her log. Completely comfortable with Kris's presence, her relaxed manner indicated that he visited often.

To my left, directly across the hall from Leah's, Elijah was still awake, and engrossed in his artwork. *Doesn't he ever sleep?* He appeared to be distant, separate from everything, as though shielded from the world around him. But I couldn't have been more wrong. Blessed and cursed, Elijah was both.

Watching him, his patience and complete focus drew me closer to his room. I wondered what rendering could inspire such devout concentration.

It was too late when I noticed Kris staring through Leah's window, shaking his head as if to say, "No!"

Elijah stood, and with the horror of a displaced autistic child, shrieked like nothing I'd ever heard.

Stepping back, I tried to stop the screaming by disappearing from view, but he continued, causing Karen and the orderly to come bolting down the hall with looks that clearly said, *"You idiot! Look what you've done!"*

Several other patients were disturbed by the outburst before the door was closed and the two went about the task of trying to calm the frightened child.

What could I say? Nothing could express the humiliation of walking the entire length of the third floor, pretending not to notice the glares from the staff.

I made sure to press the right button this time.

— — —

"Now what?" Kris asked, looking into the desperate stares of several gigantic goldfish, embedded in the icy wall of the other side. Their tail-fins infrequently fluttered behind them, as if with waning breath they struggled to fall with humility into the icy torrent between the menacing crags.

Defiant, Leah responded with a shrug. "How am I supposed to know? I don't know... All I know is we need to be *there*." She pointed to the other side.

Moving closer to the cliff's edge, Kris could see no end to its depth. "Oh child, is this what they call a bottomless pit?"

"I don't know... And that bridge looks kinda shaky..." She surveyed her left and then right, hoping to find another way across, but was distracted by the sudden formation of a cloud. Just by its appearance, it seemed like an omen, but then turned into a large circle resembling a huge smoke ring.

"Look! This *is* the way to Oz!" Leah said, but her elation was cut short by the memory of her father's firm voice declaring it an evil book. Her penitence for hiding the novel under her pillow was to endure the Reverend's recitals until morning broke. Forced to stand on a chair, she knew that if she faltered before the rooster's crow, lashes from his belt would follow.

As she stared tensely at the cloud, from within its center Jacob's voice rang like thunder. "Repent of your sins and turn to God!"

"I'm sorry father!" She wept in submission. "I'm trying not to sin! I *want* to be good! I'm *trying* to be good."

"Don't listen to him!" Kris shouted. But the preacher haunted her with the persistence of a bloodhound pursuing a desperate rabbit.

With little more to offer than what he had known in his own childhood, the Reverend ruled his family, home and church like a dictator. Above reproach, he was the law, the judge, and the jury, possessed by his self-serving interpretations of the Word of God.

All else fading to a blur, Leah stared with ghostly eyes. One-by-one the captive goldfish burst through the far cliff wall and, with screams like slaughterhouse swine, plunged into the gap. Hopeless, she repeated, "I'm sorry father! I'm sorry I'm evil…" The words echoed through the ravine, as she professed her guilt and shame to this world of her own conjuring.

Petrified, she stood staring as the sky darkened and the fish plunged like flaming boulders into the abyss below. Their terrified screams shot through the canyon, followed by explosions that rattled the deepest crevices of her torment.

"Who am I?" Jacob shouted, demanding reply.

"The Deacon of the hills," she trembled.

"That's right," he grinned with contempt. "I am the finder of wrongs, and you Leah, have been very..."

"No, Leah. Don't listen to him. Cover your ears," Kris shouted.

She placed both hands over her ears and closed her eyes, but could only think of the day her father made his proclamation...

With his Bible held high above his head, Jacob's voice resonated through the small church.

"I am the finder of evil, the deterrent to temptation, and the Deacon of these hills!"

The devoted congregation, hands high above them, shouted "Halleluiah! Praise the Lord!" But the twins held hands tightly, knowing that the sadistic reverend was capable of inflicting cruel and painful punishments.

Forbidden to watch, read or listen to anything but what he deemed appropriate, the twins had seen many changes in Jacob. They didn't understand why 'Daddy' had become 'Sir', or why things they used to do were now forbidden.

She then remembered his wrath when, only weeks after finding the hidden book, he came home unexpectedly one morning.

The credits of 'The Wizard of Oz' scrolled down the small television, as the twins, seated on either side of Naomi, fell silent.

An 'instrument of the Devil', their television was rarely used, always covered with a blanket, which was only to be removed by Jacob.

When he walked across the floor to turn it off, even Naomi trembled. With an arm around both twins, she pulled them closer. "Go play outside," she whispered. She was the one to blame.

Defiant, Leah stood. Facing her father, "It's only a movie!" she shouted.

"Only a movie?" Jacob asked. "And are my rules only rules? You and your brother go outside. I'll deal with you later." He then turned his stare to his wife, who would pay dearly for her indiscretion.

Her mother's helpless cries rang through her memory.

"Say the words." Now mounting the dark horse that had followed her across the plain, he continued, "You know you must repent. It's the only way." His eyes, like those of the steed, were frightening, unyielding. And even here, as in life, there was no haven from his cold, piercing stare.

Stepping upon her chair, she stood in the required position. "The Lord is my shepherd, I shalt not want."

―――――

After downing a carton of milk, my hands were still shaking as I returned to my room with Elijah's tormented screeches resounding in my mind. Still clothed, I sprawled out on the bed and wondered what caused him to react like that. *Was it me? Does he respond to everyone the same way? God, I need a drink.*

A knock on the door woke me early the next morning. Kathleen had come to ask about the Elijah incident.

"Good morning," she greeted. "So what happened last night? Elijah had one of his fits?"

"Yeah, you could say that," I answered groggily.

"Why were you on the third floor at that hour?"

It was much too early for an interrogation, and not to be placed on the defensive, I shot back. "I'm sorry, I didn't realize that floor was off limits after nine."

"I spoke with Dr. Feldman this morning. She had to be called to sedate Elijah after your little visit."

"My 'little visit'? Look, I'm really sorry. I got off on the wrong floor, so I went to check on Leah…"

Hearing the tone of my voice, she changed bearing. "I guess I really should've told you more about Elijah before now. We'll be meeting with Annie, Dr. Feldman, this morning. She's the head of psychology, and an interesting lady. I think you'll like her."

"So am I getting detention, or a lecture?"

"No, nothing like that. I doubt she'll even bring up last night, she's much too professional." She changed subjects. "So, how's it going? All situated?"

"I'm okay. But hey, how do I reach room service?"

"Right... Well, we have something called self-service here. You should try it sometime. Anyway, if we hurry, we might have time for a bagel. And you may wanna change out of those pants. You sleep in em?"

Closing the door behind her, "You've got ten minutes," she said.

— — —

Even in Leah's dream, the chair on which she was shamed too many times seemed out of place. But with the symbol of her suffering now there, she balanced herself until succumbing to sheer exhaustion. Her father's sermon resounded over and over in her mind, but fear of his belt, or worse, could no longer prevent her knees from buckling.

She tumbled to the snow, where she expected to feel the sting across her back, but instead heard the assuring voice of her guide. "It's okay," he whispered. "He's gone."

She raised her head to see for herself. *He is! He's gone!* From left to right, Leah looked for another crossing, then reluctantly back to the unsteady bridge. "Is there no other way?" she asked.

"Can't you just 'dream us' to the other side?" Kris responded.

"No, it doesn't work that way," she frowned, surprised that he didn't know. "We have to cross *now* then! We have to cross before he comes back!"

They were only a few feet from the bridge when Kris placed a hand on her shoulder. "Let me go first."

———

I changed into more appropriate clothes, per Kathleen's request. Knowing I had to hurry, I logged a quick recording...

"Had my first contact with Elijah last night. He's a very frightened little boy, and it didn't go too well...

Lambert's reports suggest Leah is possibly clairvoyant, and this could be something the twins share... Meeting the psychology department head this morning. Should be fun."

As I stepped into the cafeteria I saw Kathleen seated at a window table, reviewing paperwork.

After taking two bagels and pouring a cup of coffee, I sat beside her.

"Don't you have an office?" I took a bite.

"Uh huh," she responded without looking up. "Two doors before Dr. Young's."

As she continued to read and take notes, I raised my cup to take a sip. Despite my attempts to hide my shaky grasp, she raised her head and stared at my hand.

She'd never seen my shakes before, as it wasn't until after my return from the island that my drinking became a real problem.

Embarrassed, I sat the cup down as calmly as I could, but still managed to stain the white tablecloth.

"Are you okay?"

"Yeah, fine." I tried to appear collected.

"Well, you don't *look* fine. You're pale, and what's up with the shaking?"

"I dunno, maybe jet lag." I didn't want her to know the extent of my drinking, but something in her eyes told me she already knew. *Damn it, John.*

She turned back to her reports, and while she sat quietly doing paperwork, I raised the cup again, and my thoughts were soon back on the island in the South Pacific...

The day I arrived, I stepped onto the plane's pontoons, and a makeshift wooden pier.

Though it had been over a year, tropical flowers still fragranced my memory.

"I'm Matareka." The copper skinned boy began helping with my bags and I knew right away I'd like him.

"David." I extended a hand, which he shook with a bashful smile. "So you're my translator?"

"Yes," he answered. "Welcome to Lauani. Please, follow me."

A volcanic atoll east of New Zealand, the island was unspoiled by the progress of modern man. Its lagoon, lined with pristine white sand, was so clear I could see the coral on its bed, glistening in the afternoon sun.

Matareka—whom I had already decided to call Reka—led me through a gathering of the entire village. Only in his teens, his dark eyes held an ancient, primal gaze.

As I sucked on a throat lozenge, I turned to him when they began chanting, "Fakaalofa... fakaalofa."

"My people welcome you."

Bowing graciously as several children draped leis around my neck, I was excited to finally be among the revered Dreamtalkers. I didn't know then how profoundly they would affect my life.

"We should probably get going." With a glance at her watch, Kathleen brought me back to Meadowsview.

— — —

Kris stepped in front of Leah and drew a deep breath. With a foot on the first plank, he grasped the ropes cautiously. He moved forward slowly, and the crude bridge held his weight well. He then stepped onto the second and third planks.

Managing a smile, he turned to Leah and nervously encouraged her, "It's okay, come child."

The narrow bridge swayed gently from side to side, as small pieces of ice fell from it. Frightened, she looked to the outlying clouds where Jacob had appeared.

Several steps across the deep divide, they held the icy ropes and took watchful steps. "Everything will be fine," Kris assured. "Just don't look down."

"Oh God!" Leah gasped, paralyzed as she stared into the murky void.

"No!" he shouted, as he too stared into the swirling shadows which resembled a current of black tar.

Horrified by the ascending vortex, she turned around.

"No, Leah! We're too far to go back. We have to keep going!"

"Sinful child..." Jacob said with a taunting whisper, as she stood frozen, knowing too well the fury behind the familiar voice.

"Dr. Scott, dial 301." The page repeated over the public address, "Dr. Scott, 301 please."

She picked up the nearest phone. "Great." Her face went flush as she hung up and turned to the door. "It's Leah... I need to go."

"Should I go with you?"

"No. Go on to Dr. Feldman's office. It's across the hall from Dr. Young's. I'll try to come, but no guarantees."

"Okay," I agreed with a nod, but wasn't thrilled about meeting Dr. Feldman without her.

"Oh, and David, would you mind putting these on my desk?" She handed me her folders. "Two doors before Dr. Young's."

Kathleen's office walls were decorated with twelve black and white photographs, framed in shadowboxes that threw elongated shadows on the far wall. After placing the files on her desk, I stepped in front of each of the prints, stopping in front of the last picture. It was a shot of us, along with several of our friends and classmates, at a college graduation party. All of us toasting the camera, we were filled with optimism, somehow certain that our sleepless nights in the library assured us of reasonable expectations. But our exuberance wasn't what held my attention, it was the look in her eyes as she stood with her glass raised, staring at me.

A picture's worth a thousand words.

— — —

"Sinful child," the whisper repeated, as Leah looked at Kris. Now dreaming in slow motion, like a sequence of freeze-frames, she turned to the penetrating eyes behind her.

"Repent, Leah!" Dressed in white, her father's arms were outstretched. "Cast aside the curse!"

"No, Leah!" Kris shouted, "Come Child!" He was more than halfway across the bridge and frantically waved as the surge below grew stronger and began to fill the gorge.

Jacob's voice became louder, more intense. "Leah, repent and your soul will be saved!"

"No! He lies!" Kris said. "Don't listen!"

Confused, she stood petrified, wide-eyed. How could he be there? Was there no escape from him even in her dreams?

Striding past the nurse's station, Kathleen stepped through Leah's door. "What's going on?"

"Her heart-rate's out there, over two-hundred eighty beats a minute," the attending nurse answered.

"Okay, Carmen, would this be AFL, or AFib?" Kathleen asked.

"AFL," the nurse answered without hesitation.

"Good. That's right," Kathleen said. "And how do we know that?"

"The beats are rhythmic—in a sawtooth pattern." She pointed to the monitor.

"Right again. And now, how do we treat atrial flutters?"

"Um..." Carmen responded. "Beta-blockers?"

"Very good," Kathleen commended her. "We'll start with ten milligrams."

"Yes doctor," the nurse said, admiring her superior's ability to both treat and teach.

Closing her eyes, she drew upon warmer thoughts. This time the memory was of Elijah and the skill of his drawings...

"You're really good, ya know?" He was plainly gifted, and she loved him like no one else.

With an innocent expression, he looked up for several seconds, smiling before turning back to the page.

She often knew what her twin was thinking. Connected, it was as if something between them fused their thoughts together. And though most people considered him dimwitted, slow, or stupid, Leah always knew he was in another place—a refuge far away from their father's perpetual condemnations.

"Come pray! Cleanse thyself!" Jacob's eminent voice lured from behind.

She turned to her father with intensity, her eyes reflecting the burden of never ending restitution. "No!" Leah screamed and the word echoed through the chasm. Kris watched proudly as she then turned her back to the Reverend Goforth.

I was greeted by the Chief of Psychology. "Good morning, David."

"Good morning, Dr. Feldman."

"Annie." Smiling, she shook my hand.

Appearing to be in her late fifties, her gray hair was in a ponytail, and her office walls were decked out with peace signs and smiley faces, giving the room an aura of yellow and green.

"Dr. Scott's been detained," I said, trying to hide my anxiety.

"Well, that's okay. We'll have to manage without her. Please, have a seat." She gripped an earpiece of her glasses.

"She had to check on Lani."

"Lani?"

"I mean, Leah," I said.

Dr. Feldman was certainly the interesting lady Kathleen had said she was. Within moments I felt like I was the subject of the meeting, rather than meeting a new colleague.

"Tell me about you?"

"More specifically?"

"What brings you to Meadowsview, David?"

I respected her cordial manner. "The Goforth case," I answered, knowing she was well-aware of why I was there.

"Yes, that is a unique case... and what do you think of Elijah?"

Recalling the previous night, I was embarrassed. "I've only had limited contact with him so far."

"Have you looked at his sketches?"

Another person asking that question... I need to look at those drawings.

"No," I answered, feeling much the same as Kathleen must have felt about Leah's file.

"I'm really sorry about last night," I started to explain.

"It's alright, David. Autism is very difficult to understand, and Elijah's particularly unusual. He's intelligent, well above the average IQ, but so detached." She stood and walked past me, to a bookcase where she leaned closer, again gripping her glasses. "Here we go," she announced and lifted a thick hardback from an upper shelf. "I found this one quite useful in explaining Autism

Spectrum Disorder." She handed me the book.

Knowing my time at Meadowsview was limited, I had no intention of taking a crash course on autism, but I thanked her and flipped through a few pages before placing it on the desk.

I admired her polite, though efficient, demeanor, and it was easy to see how she had become the Director of Psychology at such a renowned facility.

— — —

Leah knew that Jacob would retaliate swiftly and she rushed toward Kris, at times skipping planks as she held the ropes loosely.

"Hurry!" he called out, looking past her into the furious eyes of the preacher.

Having never defied him, or turned her back for other than a beating, she felt a strange realization. Although short-lived, and in spite of certain punishment, for an instant she felt a triumphant sense of freedom.

"Go! Go! Hurry!" Kris shouted as the bridge began rocking more violently.

Stumbling to her knees, Leah gasped as she looked behind her.

Though her father had vanished, his words were louder and now came from all around them. "Wicked child!"

Regaining her footing, she reached Kris and her pulse raced as she pushed him and screamed, "Faster! Go!"

Suddenly set against a fiery crimson sky, the surge below them rose. Hell's darkness ascended through the gorge, dark bubbles bursting on its surface as it inched higher, closer to the bridge.

———

"Atrial flutter nine-twenty-two a.m.; I.V. 10mg IND." Kathleen scribbled in the log. "That's some dream," she mumbled.

"Or nightmare," Carmen said while they both watched the rapid tremble under Leah's eyelids.

———

"Leah's Glasgow Score, what do you make of that?" Annie asked, fishing to see if I'd reviewed the patient's file.

"I don't make a lot of it. She's dreaming and that's all I know. She's in another place, and, with due respect, at this point I don't think her coma score amounts to much."

— — —

Leah's screams were drowned out by her father's merciless sermon. Clenching the ropes tightly, her dream was now the nightmare the Reverend Goforth had promised sinners—and she knew she was a sinner. She watched in terror as the ebony flow began to cover the middle planks, where the bridge bowed. Catatonic, she stood only steps away from two dark bubbles which burst open, releasing a tandem of grinning demons.

"Suffer the children," Jacob rambled while, frozen in fright Leah shrieked at the sight of the terrifying forms moving closer, beaming as they grasped at her feet.

"Noooooo!" she screamed.

Leah's body convulsed, her waist arching upwards several times before she again lay flat.

The beeps that mimicked her pulse became a steady hum.

She's flat-lining. Kathleen lunged for the defibrillator.

Placing the two discs firmly on Leah's chest, "Clear," she said, to which Carmen took a step backwards.

The jolt could be heard across the hall, where Elijah and Kris both turned toward the window.

"Where is she?" Kris asked.

Without looking down, Elijah placed an index finger on his drawing. "Here," he answered, and began rocking back and forth. He then began pounding his head with his hands. *She's not evil! She's not... You're evil, father! You are!*

Kris had never 'heard' Elijah's thoughts before, but he heard them clearly now.

No. She's not evil. He placed an arm around the frightened boy, trying to calm him.

Tears streaked his face as Elijah began to erase parts of his drawing, and then angrily erased more. Bit by bit the page became lighter and his rocking ceased.

With Kris curiously watching, he erased all but the bridge, and an empty chair in the foreground. He then drew two forms huddled together safely on the other side.

— — —

Light. A single ray of sunlight penetrated the darkness,

and the sermon was silenced. The shadows disintegrated as daylight soothed the ebb and flow of Leah's terror. In the eerie calm, she and Kris completed the first crossing.

Sitting together, they quietly surveyed the frozen ravine, where not a remnant of the horror remained. But Leah knew that the demons were merely dormant and would return. They always did.

"There's still much daylight." Kris put a hand over the fist clenching his coat, and after a last gaze at the bridge, they continued westward.

Chapter 5 – Elijah

When the twins were four, Naomi convinced Jacob to let her take them shopping. A rare outing for the children, they were both in awe of the colorful trees that lined either side of the narrow road. Arching their necks as they looked through the windows of the old pickup, they sat in bewilderment while the brilliant leaves fluttered like a silent symphony around them.

Leah, who was usually a chatter box, made only infrequent comments about the sights, while Elijah merely took them in without speaking.

In town, they each held one of Naomi's hands as they entered the general store. Elijah clung to his mother's side as she instructed Leah to hold on to the cart.

They then strolled down each aisle of the small store as Naomi selected only a few items to purchase, knowing too well that her shopping budget was limited. Flour,

Crisco, sugar, she placed the necessities in the basket.

Unlike many children, who wanted this and that, and would resort to tantrums to get it, the twins were well-mannered and obedient. Even Elijah, whose autism had been diagnosed, wouldn't think of resorting to a fit for want of a toy or trinket. But they came to a small section of a center aisle where he released his mother's hand and stood looking at a box of colored pencils. With an intense stare at the label showing thirty-six colors, he stood like a mannequin.

Birthdays and Christmas were the only times the twins received gifts, especially those that weren't necessary. Even then, they were usually second-hand toys Naomi bought from thrift stores.

She watched her son with a feeling of emptiness. How could she condone a dollar and ninety-seven cents, when her budget was ten dollars? How could she explain to Jacob, who worked long hard days for the meager wages that were barely enough to pay the rent and put food on their table? Still, the look in Elijah's eyes moved her.

"Leah, do you remember where we got this?" She placed a finger on the bag of sugar.

"Yes," her daughter answered.

"Put it back."

"Okay." She smiled and placed both hands around the five pound bag. Perceptive beyond her age, she knew that this meant Elijah was getting the pencils.

Kneeling beside him, "Do you promise to take good care of them?" Naomi asked.

His smile was the answer, and she would sacrifice a million times over for the ensuing arms around her as he squeezed with all his might. Besides, she knew how to deal with Jacob.

When his son walked through the back door clutching the box, still wrapped in plastic, Jacob turned to Naomi. Without a word, she faced her husband. She understood his humility as they exchanged stares.

"He promised to take good care of them," she finally said.

"Bring them here," Jacob turned to Elijah, who hesitated, clutching the box ever closer. He then went to his father, who sat up on the couch. As Naomi and Leah watched, he took the box from his son and removed the plastic. "Leah, I need you to get some paper off my desk. Pencils aren't much good without paper, now are they?" He smiled at his son, who responded with the same bear hug he'd given Naomi in the store.

Placing her fingertips on her lips, her eyes filled with tears as she watched her husband hold their son.

Red, blue, and yellow, Elijah put the pencils on the wooden living room floor. He then placed purple, green, and orange between them, forming a circle.

One-by-one, he removed the pencils and created a perfect color wheel. It was no coincidence or matter of luck—even at the age of four he understood. No courses on color theory, freehand drawing, or portraiture could compare to the raw, natural talent that Elijah possessed. Line, form, perspective and shading, he began his first drawing with precise, deliberate strokes of a light gray pencil.

Leah sat beside him and he handed her three pencils, to which she smiled.

With the twins occupied, Naomi faced Jacob and then nodded toward their bedroom. "I'm taking my bath now."
She left the room and Jacob followed.
Instead of the nightshirt she usually wore, she removed a pale blue teddy from a hanger in their closet, knowing her husband was watching. She then turned to face him. "I'll be out in a few minutes," she said playfully. She'd planned to wear the lingerie in an effort to make up for her careless spending, but seeing him with their son reminded her of better times, and she gladly changed into the one piece of lingerie that left little to his imagination.

Two hours passed before they went back into the living room, where Elijah had drawn a flawless portrait of his twin. Both exhausted from their long overdue intimacy, they were awed by the detail in his drawing. Leah's eyes were lifelike, and her jet black hair reflected the light from the window. The rendering looked like a photograph, not the work of a four-year-old.

"I'm familiar with your writing," Annie stated matter-of-factly. "Just in case you were curious."
I nodded appreciatively, wondering what she thought of my work.
"Dreams? What a very intriguing field..." She placed an index finger on her chin.

"I enjoy it most of the time."

"I imagine so. It shows. Your theories are fascinating."

"Thank you." It was flattering that she was familiar with my work. "So, you've read one of my books?"

"Well, actually, all of them. Yes, you could say your celebrity precedes you." With an encouraging smile, she continued, "In fact, I found your latest one especially interesting." Pausing, as though not wanting to overstate the comparison, she added, "I just... well, I see similarities to The Collective Unconsciousness and wondered..."

"Right," I interrupted, knowing exactly where she was heading. "How much of my research draws from Jungian theory?"

"Well, yes, I see parallels."

"His theories are the basis for a lot of my work." I'd had this discussion before, and there was no getting around it, his research was the foundation for my studies.

"To what extent do you feel Jung contributed to your notoriety?" With the well placed question, she addressed one of my many insecurities. I could tell that she'd not only done her homework, but also read between the lines.

"Notoriety? That's an interesting way to phrase it." I reached for the thick books in front of me, unaware until then that my shakes had returned. "So how long have you been at Meadowsview?" I tried to divert her attention.

"Next month will be four years."

As I flipped through the pages, Dr. Feldman quietly watched, then asked, "And how long have you had the shakes?"

"I get them sometimes," was the only answer I could

come up with.

As Leah's temperature and pulse returned to normal, Kathleen looked through the windows and saw Elijah rocking from side to side as the janitor stood nearby. Discreetly watching, she privately admired Kris for the untiring hours he spent with the twins. Other than his flirtatious charm with the cafeteria girls, he'd kept to himself during his brief time at Meadowsview, and it puzzled her. *Why is he so involved with the twins? Nobody actually asked him to sit with the children....He's the janitor, for God's sake.* But there he was, comforting a little boy whose vacant stare and constant twitching disturbed everyone else.

Lulling himself from left to right, Elijah's olive skin seemed out of place under the fluorescent lights.

The wooden box on the table in front of him was carved by his grandfather. Lifelike, the intricate detail of a barn owl was skillfully etched in its lid.

Each day Dr. Feldman tried to persuade him to talk about the box and what it contained, but he remained silent, sharing it with only Leah. She knew what was inside of his box, just as she knew what was inside of him. His best friend, protector, and cellmate, they shared everything, and no one, including their oppressive father, could prevent them from sharing even their dreams...

Leah lay on the bunk above him as they huddled close

to the wall in their small bedroom.

"Elijah?" she spoke softly, making sure not to invoke the Reverend's wrath. "Elijah…"

"I'm awake." He always answered in the same monotone whisper.

"Come with me to Oz," she said. "Let's fly away!"

Seeing his sister's tiny fingers reach between the wall and bed frame, he raised a small hand and clutched them tightly, listening to her stories while, in the next room, Jacob rehearsed frightening sermons of eternal suffering.

"We'll follow the yellow brick road." Her southern accent was strong. "But we'll *nevah* come back!"

"Okay," he smiled as they both imagined being anywhere else.

The stories only ended when Elijah's hand lost its grasp and Leah knew that he was dreaming. She then hurried to sleep, knowing they would soon be together, away from their private hell.

To Elijah, his sister was an angel, and it was she who bore the scars of endless times she'd come to his defense while Naomi stood helpless. He trembled at the memory of other nights, nights he lay staring into the small kitchen while Leah stood like a crucifix on her wooden chair.

He helped her endure their father's treacherous punishment. Closing his eyes, he silently asked, *Leah, remember Oz?*

Yes... He heard her answer as though she was speaking into his ear. *We'll go see the Wizard, and we'll ask if we can stay!*

With the narrow icy bridge now far behind, Leah looked up at Kris, her white knuckles wrapped firmly around his fingers. "I'm so tired…so, so tired."

Until then, they hadn't noticed the random patches of green all around them. "Look!" she called out, releasing his fingers. "Scarecrow! Look!"

Leah needed springtime, and so it now flourished in her dream, as newly sprouting blades of grass soon sprang from beneath the white-capped mounds.

"Grass! And Scarecrow… trees!"

Straying from the path and into an open meadow, Kris looked briefly behind them, to the distant white dunes which now obscured the icy bridge.

Under a blue sky they both fell to the earth and rested in the warmth of a shimmering sun.

Seeing calmer faces across the hall, the janitor assured, "Everything's alright now."

Elijah, drawing in hand, stumbled to his dresser, where he placed it on top of the others. For several moments he lined up the edges of his pictures, his only sense of jurisdiction in a world that frightened and deceived him. *Perfect,* he thought, finally satisfied that the stack met his symmetrical requirements. Staring through the window, he looked briefly at Kris and then again through the glass.

Kris placed a clean white page on the table in front of the boy's chair. *Show me… Show me where she's going.*

Show me... Looking into the savant's young eyes he wondered what testament was buried beneath them.

I will show you, Elijah responded and returned to his seat.

"Good," Kris answered and, with an encouraging nod, finished, "You draw something and I'll come back later."

Without reply, he grasped the pencil, staring at the empty sheet on which he would soon detail another glimpse of his sister's journey.

Kris left him with a last thought. *Everything will be okay.*

With a disjointed smirk, Elijah merely glanced across the table and then down at the page, where the image was already emerging in his mind.

Annie was careful not to put too fine a point on my shakes. "Your tests, how are they conducted?"

I cleared my throat. "Typically, the subject is awake both before and after the workup."

She nodded. "But how do you... *do* your tests?" With genuine interest, she listened to an abbreviated description of my practices.

"Everything's fed simultaneously into a program... an amazing program." I raised an eyebrow. "My brother designed the software." I was proud of John's efforts and had to admit that he definitely knew his way around a computer.

"But what does the program do? I mean, do you actually watch what they're dreaming on a monitor?" She seemed embarrassed by the sound of her question.

"No. The impulses aren't interpreted as pixels, but rather as mathematical composites."

"Okay, now you've really lost me. I'm sorry. I have no idea what you're talking about."

"Put it like this, what if an equation told if you dreamt in color or black and white? Or if it was day or night?"

"Go on," she urged.

"I'm not saying we can isolate every thought, we're still years away from that, but, for instance, about four months ago I did a full workup on a friend of mine, a real critic... He pretty much told me it couldn't be done, but after reviewing the data I told him he dreamt he was wearing a red cap in a sold out stadium."

"And?"

"He said he pitched a no-hitter for the Reds."

"Impressive, but I guess what I need to know is what do you need from us, or me. What do you need me to do?"

"I'd like to run some tests with Leah."

"Of course."

"A complete breakdown," I added.

"Well, I don't know what 'complete breakdown' means, but this is my in-box." She pointed to a plastic tray on the desktop. "I'll need something in writing. Tell me what you need and how we can assist you."

"I'll need to place sensors on their scalps... "

"Write it down," she said. "Meadowsview requires any non-standard procedures follow specific protocol. And the kind of patient access you're requesting calls for Level Six clearance. I think there's a total of twelve people in the entire building with that security level.

Fortunately," she grinned, "I'm one of them. But, again, just write it down."

"Got it," I said. "Tomorrow. I'll give it to you tomorrow."

"Tomorrow morning would be great. We really can't move forward until I sign off on it."

"I'll have something for you tomorrow morning."

"David, we both know this case has remarkable potential."

"Potential?" I wasn't sure how to respond. "Well, yes, I guess it does have a lot of implications. But I've never done a workup on someone in a coma."

"Yes, of course. But, just between us, I'm looking forward to your test, and the results." Pausing, she gave me a curious gaze, and started to finish. "Do you think it's possible that Elijah and Leah..." she stopped mid-sentence, but I knew what she was thinking.

"Dream sharing isn't uncommon," I said. "We've all probably done it." Though it was the most disputed aspect of my theory, I firmly believed it.

"So you think everyone shares dreams?"

"Not everyday, but yes. Our subliminal minds receive and transmit signals."

"WTF?"

"Exactly." I smiled and then, seeing her glance at her watch, stood to go.

"It should be interesting, and please let me know what you need. Write it down."

She showed me to the door, where she extended her hand. "Its been a pleasure meeting you, David. We'll talk again soon."

"Likewise. So, I think I'll go see how Kathleen's doing with Leah."

"Yes. Good. And welcome aboard. I look forward to working with you. Oh, don't forget the books." She handed them to me, then, before opening the door, whispered, "And if you ever want to talk about your drinking, or anything else..."

As I walked across the polished marble of Meadowsview's main floor, my thoughts drifted again to Polynesia...

The tropical sunlight beamed down as the palm trees gently listed in the wind.

Reka translated the elder's words as I recorded their stories of shared visions.

Shyly smiling, the children circled around and laughed when I occasionally replayed bits of the video.

Gracious in gifting me with bright flowers and tropical fruits, the islanders gained my complete admiration and affection. They were beautiful people, unspoiled by the complex enormity of modern machines and sciences. I felt as if I'd stepped back in time, to an island Eden far away from the mundane suburb where I e-mailed this and microwaved that.

Many of them were reserved, but one child, one little girl, was particularly shy and curiously watched with an innocent smile. Always standing behind the others, she seemed to have a full grasp on the reasons I was there.

Her name was Lani.

When I stepped from the elevator Kathleen was walking toward me.

"How'd it go?"

"Okay, I guess."

"And what's that?" She looked down at the books.

"More reading," I smirked.

"How's Leah?"

"She arrested, but she's okay now…she's fine now…" She was at a loss.

"Well, she has the best doctor possible."

"Thanks. So how did you like Annie?"

"She's groovy, man." I smiled and gripped an imaginary earpiece.

Kathleen smiled too. "Oh, I know, and when she looks up over the rims I always feel like she sees right through me... She really is a sweet lady though, and also has a genius IQ." Her respect for the psychologist was obvious as she went on, "Seriously David, she's one of the best in her field, and I'm hoping the two of you together will be able to sort a few things out."

———

With complete focus, Elijah sat at his drawing table and began a new illustration. His small fingers loosely gripped the pencil, and in long, deliberate strokes he began to give life to the white page.

Usually hauntingly quiet, in the days they'd been at Meadowsview he'd been lost in the shuffle, patiently drawing most of the time. His artwork, two daily sessions with Dr. Feldman, and infrequent visits to the cafeteria vending machines or main floor lobby, occupied the majority of his time. The nurses looked in on him regularly and made sure he was fed and bathed, but other than Kris, who checked on him as often as he could, the staff was unsure of how to handle the child.

Executed with precision that even da Vinci would envy, his finished pieces could almost pass as photographs. Beyond talented, he was touched by God. Though some called him a savant, others an idiot, few could see past the void awkwardness that reminded them of their own mortality.

He continued to draw until a small black ant wandered across the page, then lifted his pencil and stared curiously at the errant insect.

"There's someone else you should be introduced to." Kathleen pointed to the other end of the hall and decided, ready or not, it was time for me to meet Elijah.

"Okay," I answered hesitantly. "But do you think he's ready for me?"

"Well, there's only one way to find out." She led me to his room.

"I'll go in first and see how things look," she said, wanting to avoid another scene like the night before.

"Good idea."

When we reached his window she hesitated, then slowly opened the door and stepped inside.

"Elijah…" she whispered, making sure not to startle him. She then tactfully stepped to the far side of his table.

"Elijah, there's someone I want you to meet."

He looked down without response.

"There's someone who wants to talk to you."

Still, no response.

"His name's David and he just wants to look at your drawings." At this, the boy glanced at her and then to the window through which I watched with a nervous smile.

His face, which had been blank and emotionless, became tense as he saw me, but Kathleen was quick to assure him. "Elijah, his name's David and he won't hurt you… he just wants to see your drawings."

Looking anywhere but into her eyes, he returned to his work as Kathleen signaled, and I cautiously stepped inside the room.

"Elijah, this is David."

He flinched several times without looking up.

"Hello." I approached and saw that he was playing with a black ant. "What ya got there?" I asked, watching him maneuver his eraser around the insect.

He pretended not to hear. With both elbows on the table, he tried to completely tune us out while playing with the ant.

I inched closer and was instantly able to see his brilliance. The drawing was only partially completed, but there they were, two figures on a road shadowed by trees.

Repeatedly wiping his nose and scratching his earlobe, his head was tilted to one side and right hand hovered strangely near his face. His left hand loosely held the pencil as he toyed with the moving speck, careful not to touch it.

Elijah was perplexing, and I was drawn not only to his

artistic ability, but also his reverence. This was truly a child who wouldn't harm an ant.

After a moment, Kathleen broke the silence. "Can we look at your drawings?"

His flinching became more frequent, but having surely heard her, he maintained his silence.

She then nodded to a chest of drawers on which he kept his drawings.

I quietly stepped across the floor and noticed that the staff had gone to great lengths to accommodate the child. The room had been carefully decorated to suit the liking of any typical twelve-year-old boy, but Elijah was far from typical, so certain precautions had also been taken. The furniture had rounded corners and edges, his lamps were wired directly into the outlets, and a small wooden bookshelf was bolted into the wall.

The drawings were stacked with their edges perfectly lined up, and as I looked at the one on top I was immediately compelled into his world. Urgent. Graphic. His work was nothing less than that of a prodigy.

The depiction of two wintry figures kneeling at the far side of an icy bridge was striking, and with meticulous shading, he'd filled the snow-laden crevices of a deep gorge. Although parts had been erased or left white, the detail was lifelike, and with a surreal twist, he'd put a vacant wooden chair on the near side of the landscape.

So far, my first meeting with him had gone better than expected, so I decided to test the waters. "Is this a chair?" I asked.

He glanced at me through the corners of his eyes. With pencil in hand he then delivered the wayward ant to the windowsill, while she and I exchanged bewildered looks, wondering what was next.

"Leah's chair," he spoke in a weird voice, sounding somewhat like a parrot.

Contact. Looking at Kathleen, who was also surprised, I remembered what Kris had said. "And is this Leah over here?" I pointed to the far side of the bridge.

Silence again filled the room as I met Kathleen's encouraging stare.

Elijah, rocking back and forth, finally confirmed, "Yes," and fell gracelessly to his bed. "Sleep now, sleep now…sleep now…" he repeated, then curled up on top of the blankets.

With his retreat, and not wanting to push our luck, we said goodbye and Kathleen left the door slightly ajar behind us.

"Does he ever get out of here?" I asked, thinking that in a different environment he might open up and answer a few questions.

"Not that I know of. Why?"

"Maybe we can take him out sometime?"

"What?" She responded in disbelief. "Are you crazy?"

"The only way he'll open up is if we gain his complete trust." I answered assuredly, as though I was now a communications expert. "And, we're kind of on a timeline here, aren't we?" I asked pointedly.

"Yes, of course, and I'm impressed that he spoke to you, but look, they've been here several days and he's hardly said a word. I've tried, Annie's tried..."

"But have you tried anywhere other than that room? I mean, do you actually think a few toys and an NFL comforter make it anything less than a sterile prison?"

"And do you really think you can take him outside with paper and pencils, bounce him on your knee a few times and he's going to magically open up and tell you everything?"

"Do you have a better idea?"

"No, but David, he's autistic, it's not like he communicates very well in the first place."

"God, I'd forgotten what a cynic you are."

"Don't even start... All I'm saying is he isn't gonna let you push him on the merry-go-round, so don't delude yourself."

"Point taken," I answered. "But I think it's worth a try."

"Look, I've got patients to see and I'm buried in paperwork." She walked me to the elevator. "That went pretty well, and I'll see what I can do..."

"'See what you can do?' You mean you'll think about it?"

"I *will* think about it, David." She playfully tossed her hair. "But right now I'm back to being Kathleen Scott, doctor extraordinaire." She grinned and returned to her patients.

My meeting with Elijah having gone well, I stood staring through my fourth floor window.

Autumn appeared to have fully arrived overnight. Restless, the leaves were colored in earthen hues and would soon join the already fallen scatterings along the meadow's edge.

What's the chair represent? Who's the other figure? Is

it him? I didn't have the answers, but at least felt like I now knew a few of the questions.

After looking through the window for several minutes I fell on the bed and closed my eyes.

— — —

The scent of spring surrounded her as Leah was awakened by a gentle hand.

"Okay," Kris whispered, "I thought you were Dorothy, not Sleeping Beauty."

She opened her eyes and rose to her feet, then stretched her arms high above her.

After a few steps she picked up a small branch and waved it like a magic wand. Refusing to look to the past, she lined the sides of the trail with brilliant hues.

A different kind of sun warmed the air and shot rays of light across the passage, reminding her of another passage, a trail near their house, where she and Elijah laughed as they ran to see the whistling train...

Hurrying through the door, she called, "Elijah! Come see the train!"

He stumbled across the small back porch and down a well-worn path through the woods. Frequently falling, he always got back on his feet. "The train. The train," he repeated.

From atop a large granite boulder, they stared anxiously at the tunnel beyond the suspension bridge. It was rare to see Elijah smile, and Leah cherished the memories of sitting with him on the rock. "Maybe someday we'll go with them!" She placed an arm around her brother, his face beaming with anticipation.

Within moments the train came through the tunnel, its whistle blowing as it spanned the deep Appalachian gap.

"Chooo-chooo," he mimicked and rocked from side to side in his sister's arms.

They were moments of levity, when they could at least imagine far away places, but always too soon the train disappeared, taking with it Elijah's smile.

She waved her wand like a paintbrush with which she conjured a flowing stream. And where it crossed their path ahead, under a bridge of purple and orange stones, she covered its banks with green moss.

Twenty or so feet in length, the bridge arched slightly in the middle. Pristine. Inviting. It was much different than the ice bridge, and she was anxious to cross. On solid footing, she began across the stones, but paused when she saw her reflection in a shallow pool below. As a light mist rose from the water, her image changed into that of her mother.

"Meet me where hope lives," she said clearly. Naomi's dark eyes rippled in the currant, until completely vanishing downstream.

"Mommy, don't go. Come back!" Leah plead, to no avail.

Meet me where hope lives? What does that mean? Where does hope live? Looking a last time into the stream, she let the stick fall from her hand and continued along the trail.

With Kris following only steps behind her, they were soon given a choice. As in a poem she had once read, the road ahead of them forked. To the left, the path led into a deep forest of hunter green and the trees curved oddly, forming a tunnel through which yellow rays of light sporadically broke through. To the right, evergreens stood firm beneath the shadow of a mountain fortress. It was from there that they heard the whisper of a young girl—the same voice she had heard before. "Beware of false prophets."

The left path was diminutive compared to the stately pines lining the right, but its colors were alluring as it hypnotically rotated clockwise. Weighing her options, Leah turned once again to the fortress, where the voice repeated, "Beware of false prophets, they lie and will call you away."

"Which way?" she asked, looking to the fortress, and then to the inviting road less taken.

"This is your dream, shouldn't *you* decide?"

"I," she stood in doubt. "I'm not sure. I don't know which way..."

When the sound of a train's whistle suddenly shot through the south passageway, "This way!" she shouted, turning away from the whisper, as she was drawn to the familiar wail.

The branches slowly twirled, forming a beguiling entry through which she began walking. "The train! Scarecrow? Where are you Kris?"

Alone, Leah stood petrified as she watched the tree branches methodically close behind her, separating her from her guide and leaving no choice but to continue through the tunnel. *Why did he leave me alone?*

Memories came again, this time from the previous

summer, when a sweltering sun heated the canyon where she and Elijah wandered.

Waiting patiently for her unwieldy twin, who always trailed, she pointed. "I bet there's a pot of gold over there, under your bridge, Elijah!"

Elijah's bridge! He looked up smiling, his eyes filled with wonder as his sister ran ahead and sat in a tire tied to an old oak tree.

"I'm coming," he assured.

"It's okay." His limitations weren't his fault, and Leah knew better than anyone that her twin was blessed in other ways.

Elijah, she thought, turning back with a look he knew well.

Yes? He answered without speaking, *I'm coming.*

That's your bridge Elijah, and someday you'll cross it! The thrill in his eyes made her smile. *I know you like that idea!*

Go without me today, he responded, but she never went further, choosing instead to stay and 'talk-talk', as they called their silent conversations. Under the blistering West Virginia sun, he continued. *Go on. You can go further without me.* In their talk-talk Elijah was filled with expression, unlike the monosyllabic manner in which he spoke aloud.

Leah peered past the bridge and briefly considered continuing alone, but their mother's voice then rang through the gorge. "Children, come for supper."

Like a carnival attraction, the colorful cylinder drew her inside and she walked through the passage, mystified by the swirling colors. A few steps further, daylight revealed a familiar structure on the other side, and Leah realized that she was inside the tunnel to Elijah's bridge.

Many times she'd sat on the boulder and imagined standing precisely where she now stood, but her elation was sliced by the shrill whistle of an approaching locomotive. The ground beneath her shook as she looked behind, where the branches that had forced her down the path began to slowly unravel, revealing a portal through which she could see the oncoming train. "Oh, God!" she cried and ran toward the light.

It was louder than a whisper. "David. David. Wake up, David." Lani woke me from a dreamless sleep, and I quickly sat up in the bed. Looking around the room, I hesitated before turning the tape recorder on, then stepped into the bathroom, where I splashed my face with cold water.

"Elijah's bridge." The words came from the small cassette player on the nightstand. I looked behind me and then turned back to the mirror where, resurrected from far away, Lani stared directly into my eyes. "His vision will lead you." Her lips moved, but her voice came from behind, as though the device was some sort of translator.

I tried to dismiss her reappearance, but Lani's stare was paralyzing.

"David," she said angelically. "Don't be afraid… it's where you'll find redemption."

In the immediate blink of an eye, the apparition disappeared, and my voice came from the recorder.

"Lambert's reports suggest Leah is possibly clairvoyant..."

It's where I'll find redemption? What does that mean? Elijah's bridge... his visions...

Trembling, I dried my face, then walked to the nightstand to turn off the tape recorder. And after several deep breaths, I stood staring across the meadow, where the distant clouds hung gracefully above the Vermont countryside.

At that moment, a sense of clarity overcame me.

With each appearance, Lani was somehow weaving me deeper into the fabric of the Goforth Situation.

Chapter 6 – Naomi

The granddaughter of a spiritual leader, Naomi possessed the gift of clairvoyance, and was highly regarded by her people, who called her Go Tsa-gi... Knows Dreams.

Olive skinned, tall and slender, she was shy and soft-spoken, but also poised and confident. When she said something, it was because she had something to say.

Considered a prophet among the Cherokee, she was thought to be a witch by many of the townspeople, who feared her ability to predict the future.

Gifted beyond question, her sensitive manner surrounded her with an aura of lightness that drew her people's affection.

Only her grandfather understood the emotional burden of her foresight. Many times he'd seen frightening things —things he was without the power to change—and he knew too well that along with 'telling' came futility and hopelessness. It was a talent he often wished that he and his cherished granddaughter didn't have.

From early childhood her dreams were taken seriously, even to the extent that she regularly attended meetings of the tribal council. Her visions guided their decisions, and she served them devotedly, until she met Jacob. But he was different then.

———

It was early summer, Naomi was nineteen, and Jacob twenty-three, with one year remaining in college.

In no hurry to return home to his vindictive father, Jacob drove through West Virginia on his way back to Vermont.

In a small town north of Huntington, he pulled into a small convenience store. There he noticed Naomi ignoring the cat-calls of two scrawny teens as she walked past the pumps toward a trail leading into a grove of trees.

Having never seen such beauty, it was love at first sight for Jacob, and his stare caught her attention as she glanced at him, then quickly looked away.

The whistles and remarks from the pickup continued, but his six-foot-four frame was not to be challenged when he spoke up. "That's enough, boys."

Quickly finishing, they left, and Naomi smiled before disappearing into the dense woods.

He went inside the small market. "That girl, do you know her?" he asked the attendant behind the counter.

"What girl?" the long-haired clerk responded with a southern twang, looking as though he was completely bored.

"The one that was just in here."

"Ohhhh," he grinned. "She's quite a looker, huh?"

Jacob nodded.

"That's Naomi Snow." More animated, he continued, "But you don't want none of that. She's a witch! Trust me, you don't want none of her or her people."

Jacob merely smirked and went to the narrow footpath.

"Naomi," he said, jogging down the trail which was partly obscured by thick undergrowth.

"I've been waiting for you, Jacob."

Stunned, he stood looking into her black eyes. "How do you know my name?"

"How do you know *mine*?" She continued further into the woods. She had known for a long time that he was coming, and that his arrival would change her life, but Naomi couldn't foresee the extent to which the stranger's appearance would affect her future. Curiously, she was without the ability to predict much when it came to Jacob —some things were clear, but most were foggy.

"Wait. Really. How did you know my name?"

"Lucky guess." Smiling over her shoulder, she stepped gingerly over a fallen branch and brushed the black hair from her brow.

Trailing her through the woods, Jacob was stricken by her radiance. *And how did she know my name?*

Unkempt, the yard was littered with transmission parts, and covered by knee-high grass that partially submersed an old rusty pickup.

"Can I see you again?" he whispered as they came to the back steps of her family's modest home.

Naomi couldn't decline the invitation. Pure, and naive, she'd seen him in her dreams, and in those dreams there were always infant twins.

"Do you believe in fate?" she asked.

"Yes."

"Then yes," she said, placing a foot on the first wooden step to her back porch.

Looking over her shoulder, "Your spare tire needs air. You should look at it," she added.

Caught off guard by the out-of-the-blue statement, "I'm sure it's fine," he said.

Naomi merely grinned as her mother opened the door with disapproving eyes.

"Wait. When? Where?"

"Tomorrow. Five o'clock. The diner." With a curious smile, she went inside, and the door was quickly closed behind her.

Jacob checked into the local motel, where he looked through his window and saw the sign across the street, *Tom's Diner.*

He arrived promptly at five, and all eyes were upon him when he entered the small cafe. Sitting at a booth near the window, he was surprised when the metal doors to the kitchen opened and Naomi, clad in a white apron, stepped through.

"I'm sorry, I have to cover for a few minutes. Would you like something to drink?"

"A cold glass of water would be great."

She turned around and Jacob discreetly admired the curves under her colorful summer dress.

After a few minutes she again came through the doors, this time minus the apron and holding a glass of water.

"Here ya go." She placed the glass in front of him and sat across the table.

"How did you know my name?"

She quickly sat back and changed subjects. "So what brings you here?"

"Summer," he responded. "I'm on my way home."

Many of the town's people objected to interracial mixing.

Naomi, unaffected by the rude stares, just ignored the meddling townsfolk. Jacob, on the other hand, abruptly spoke up. "Is there something I can help you with?" He looked insistently around the diner as the old men at the counter, and other patrons, turned back to their meals and menus, reproved by the man who would later become the Reverend Jacob Goforth.

"Would you like dinner?"

"No. I have to cook for my family." Seeing his disappointment, she added, "But we could go to the park for awhile."

―――――

Drawn to her in a way he'd never known, he glanced at her shoes as they left the diner, noticing that they were well-worn, with small holes at the toes. But when she smiled it was from deep within, as though, in spite of hardship, she had a genuine appreciation for life. While he was merely going through the motions of living, she was living, finding joy in the beauty of a sunset and warm summer breeze.

Her dark hair blew in the wind as Jacob pushed Naomi on the park swing, thinking of the long haul which would take him far away from the hills of West Virginia.

"So let me guess," she said. "A rich daddy who was never really involved in anything you did, but wants you to run the family business..." She could tell so much from his leather loafers and clean fingernails.

"Business? Try *three* businesses—two maple syrup producers and an import-export. And yes, he was always too busy for me. I was the only kid on my Little League team whose dad never came to a game."

With her curfew approaching, they began toward the winding road which led to her home.

"I have to leave soon. I'm already expected back in Vermont."

"I know. But I'll still be here tomorrow, and the day after that, and the day after that." Placing her palm inside his, Naomi turned to Jacob. "And you'll be back," she confidently added.

The next morning Jacob left his room key at the motel counter and began the long drive home. The sun hadn't yet risen as he started down the winding road, thinking of nothing but Naomi.

On the outskirts of town a front tire blew. *Damn—just what I need.* He pulled to the shoulder, where he drove until coming to a dirt clearing wide enough to get off the pavement.

Grasping the spare by the inner rim, he dropped it on the sod. *Great. Two flats...* He then remembered Naomi's warning. *"Your spare tire needs air."*

Leaning against the car door, Jacob viewed the dense forest lining the narrow road, and wondered if he was leaving too soon. *And how did she know my name?*

———

One day became two, and two became three, as Jacob stayed in Cabell County, courting the mysterious Naomi Snow.

His father wasn't pleased when he finally called from West Virginia.

"You will come *home*! That's what you will do, son." The decisive tone was familiar to Jacob, who responded similarly.

"I'll come when I'm damned well ready!"

"Either be here by this weekend, or don't bother coming." Joseph hastily ended their conversation with unforeseen permanence, as the connection was cut and he didn't hear from Jacob again until several weeks later, when Naomi was pregnant.

Immediately renouncing his only son, the bigoted Joseph was enraged. "It's bad enough that you conceive a child out of wedlock, but with an indian? Consider yourself disowned." The statement was brief and irreversible.

Naomi's kin, while somewhat more civil, were equally disappointed. Many of her people were of mixed blood and to them it didn't matter, but among the full-bloods there was an unspoken understanding—they were expected to marry within their tribe and perpetuate the legacy of their ancestors. And Naomi was full-blood.

More than a summer's rain or winter's snow, she was timeless, and Jacob's love for her was true. He was moved by her gentle nature, and through Naomi he was able to define happiness.

After renting a modest home near a deep gorge, they were married in the county courthouse amid judgmental gazes. Naomi could no longer disguise the first trimester of her pregnancy.

On their way home, she stated with certainty, "You will have a daughter first, and then a son." Staring into his sober eyes, she finished, "And you will preach of God."

Autumn came and passed, and the gripping chill of a harsh winter had finally subsided when she went into labor on a Tuesday in early spring.

Eyes opened, Leah came into the world kicking and screaming, and Elijah quietly followed.

Bundled in white blankets, she held her infant twins at her breasts. "They're beautiful."

Tears streaked Naomi's cheeks while Jacob stood

beside her, clutching her hand, and overcome by the birth of their children.

"Yes," he whispered, watching his daughter, nestled close to her mother, as his son stared into the fluorescent lights.

Naomi knew from the first look in their eyes that her children were different. Prodigious. Touched by God.

When the twins were four, Elijah was diagnosed as autistic, and spent several hours each day drawing at the dining room table.

"He's gonna draw a train, Mommy!" Scribbling crude blue trees on her own page, Leah admired her brother's skill.

"How do you know?" Naomi asked, looking curiously at the blank sheet of paper.

"Because he told me," she answered with a smile and tilt of her head. "I wish I was good too."

They both then watched as Elijah effortlessly started with gray metal wheels, and put a train on its tracks.

"But I didn't hear him say anything," Naomi said.

Continuing her scrawls, Leah faced her. "Cause he didn't say it with his lips."

Naomi closed her eyes, and drew a deep breath. There had been several signs before, but she was now certain that she had passed the talent of telling to the twins.

In her blood, and in the blood of her children, it was an ability that she would help them to develop, but also a curse she would try to help them to understand.

Humbled by poverty, Jacob worked odd-jobs to support his family, knowing that without the help of Naomi's kin they couldn't make ends meet. Too stubborn to contact his father, the first years in West Virginia took a toll on his pride, but also revealed the nature of the hills people, whose strength and loyalty he admired.

Hired to paint a small church, he quietly listened each day as the devout preacher rehearsed his sermons, shouting scriptures which echoed through the building. Moved by the old man, Jacob started reading the New Testament, and the family began attending the fiery lectures of Reverend Meade, who became a frequent visitor, often bringing clothes and canned foods from the church's donations.

"I still think you should finish that degree, Jacob," he said, smiling at the twins, who were now five. "It's only one more year. You could probably finish at Marshall."

"I should've finished it five years ago."

"But you didn't," the old man grinned, adding, "and you should never think about the *I should haves.* Think about the *I wills.* I should've been rich instead of good looking." He winked at Leah, who turned to Jacob.

"I wanna be rich too, Daddy." Smiling innocently, she turned back to the gray-haired preacher she adored.

"I guess you'll do it when you get around to it... but if you don't, the other offer's still on the table." He looked at Jacob as Naomi turned around curiously.

"What offer?" she asked, knowing that the Reverend Meade's wife was ill and Jacob was the congregation's choice to become their faithful leader.

"The Reverend thinks I might be ready to try my hand at preaching."

"And what do you think?" She turned back to the sink, closed her eyes, and thanked God for her prophesy. She already knew the answer.

"I think I'd like to give it a try," he said.

"Preacher. Reverend. We all called him a different name." Three months later Jacob placed his hand on the casket, eulogizing the father figure who had lost his wife to cancer only a month before. "I called him friend." He looked to each corner of the church, remembering the first time he heard Reverend Meade deliver God's Word in an empty room, preaching as if Jacob's soul alone was worth redemption.

"I see some who attend Sunday services, and some who attend Wednesdays, but everywhere I see lives touched by his generosity and courage. And in a world needing faith, my friend was one of the most faithful... Please, bow your heads with me... Father, we give You an angel. We give You Nathanial Meade, one of Your most loyal servants. A man who walked in Your light and delivered Your Word without question or expectation. A man who dedicated his life to Your honor." Looking to the vaulted ceiling with his arms high above him, Jacob addressed the standing room only crowd. "We know Nathanial's with You, because he never left Your side."

"Amen," the congregation followed.

His first year as the leader of the church, Jacob was a rock. His sermons were engrossing, and were delivered with bone-chilling volume. Admired and respected by his flock, Reverend Goforth was as highly regarded as his mentor.

"Repent!" When his gray eyes roamed from pew to pew, the congregation knew that they were sinners, and that God was only so forgiving.

The twins were seven, and Jacob had embraced his roll as leader of the church.

While Naomi's time was divided between the children and evenings at the diner, he spent long hours rehearsing his sermons. Intimacy between them was rare, and he was different. Control. Power. The things he resented the most in his father, now consumed him.

"I miss the old Daddy," Leah said, remembering other times, when Jacob read to them and carried her on his shoulders. She remembered the father he was before his rise in the church changed him.

"I know, sweetheart," Naomi said. "I miss the old Daddy too." With a loving smile, she stroked Leah's hair and stared blankly through the window.

Confused, she didn't understand why Jacob was different. And to make things worse, she had been having dreams of an old boyfriend. *Why? Why now?* she wondered. *I haven't seen him in so long...*

Both innocent, she and Robert had never exchanged anything more than a kiss all those years ago, but Naomi envisioned his arms around her. She remembered his boyish smile, and the days they spent walking through the woods. She also remembered his grief-stricken eyes when she told him of her telling that his family would move away.

But *these* dreams were different than those she'd had when she was younger. These were filled with emotions she'd never known, and she nervously anticipated his arrival. There was no use in trying to fight it—he *would* appear. And on a rainy day in April, he did.

The diner was closed, and Naomi was seated at the booth where she and Jacob had sat eight years earlier. Tormented by her prophesy, she stared through the window with tears streaking her face. She thought of the twins, and Jacob. How could she do this? Surely, if she prayed hard enough, God would give her the strength to resist temptation. *Please, let them be just normal dreams,* she plead. But it was too late, she had foreseen her destiny.

As she stood to go home, a truck pulled up to the curb. Her heart stopped beating as she watched Robert quick-step through the rain to the front door. Finding it locked, he leaned against the glass, smiling when he saw her.

Drawing several deep breaths, she faced him with anguished eyes, and finally unlocked the door.

"Surprised?" he asked.

"No, Bobby," she whispered. "I knew you were coming."

"I would've called but..."

"But you were afraid I'd leave."

"Yes," he responded. "I was afraid you'd leave."

"How did you know I was here?" she asked. "Mom

told you? And did she also tell you that I have children?"

"Yes, twins," he answered. "And that you married a preacher."

"I did. Yes. And we have children."

He was at least six inches taller than when she'd last seen him, and the wiry boy had disappeared. Six-two, with a muscular build, Robert had completely changed. His hair, which used to be as long as hers, was now short, cut in a contemporary style. Blue jeans had been replaced with slacks, and his old denim jacket was now a dark wool coat. No longer innocent, he had become a man, and they both knew that his presence was more than a cordial visit.

For several days, Robert made discreet after-hour trips to the diner.

Torn between fidelity and a desire that she'd never known, Naomi tried to change her fate, but knew that her efforts were futile.

Once filled with life, in some ways he was still very much the boy she'd grown up with, but Bobby had changed. His years in the army had made him tense, uneasy. She could see that his time in Afghanistan had dimmed the light in his eyes. Still, he made her smile, and on a late spring night when he came to call, her destiny also came calling.

Three days later, on her way to the diner, Naomi stopped at the church. Kneeling at the altar, she thought she was there alone. *Forgive me.* She faced the wooden cross that stretched from the floor to the ceiling. *Please, forgive me.*

When Jacob entered through a side door, she was surprised, stunned.

"Where are the twins?" she asked.

"With your family. Everything okay?" He stood just inside the door, assessing the sight of his wife in tears.

She brushed her cheeks, hoping he hadn't seen her crying, but he had.

Everything made sense to him—the chill in their bedroom, her blank gazes, the absence of laughter.

"Yes," she lied, trying to muster a convincing smile. "I'm just worried about my aunt."

Knowing better, Jacob didn't respond. It was as if his chest, along with the heart inside it, fell to the floor. He wanted to ask so that she would lie—he would rather she lie than confirm the unbearable truth.

The silence, her avoidance of eye contact, the signs were undeniable. And when she finally faced him, the truth was clear. Naomi couldn't hide her guilt and shame. *If only they had been just normal dreams...*

No, he thought. *No. Not Naomi.* In an instant, a light inside of Jacob was extinguished, and in time his pain would turn into a rage that would devour his very soul.

Chapter 7 – Wednesday

Leah's eyes moved in rapid sequence from side to side, and with a rhythmic change, up and down. Having watched her several times, Kris was familiar with the pattern—four counts to the side, three up and down.

It was time to finish the third floor. "Back to work, ladies," he said as he left the room.

"See ya, Kris," Rebecca responded.

He looked through Elijah's window and started to walk past, not wanting to disturb him, but something this early morning compelled him to go in.

Usually facing the wall when he slept, Elijah was facing the door.

He looks so much like Leah, Kris thought, and took several steps across the floor.

He then noticed another similarity. *Four counts to the side, three up and down.*

I opened my eyes, thinking of Lani. Her latest appearance was particularly disturbing. I kept picturing her face and hearing the words, "It's where you'll find redemption."

Impulsively, I put both feet on the floor and decided to look at Elijah's drawings.

Hoping to find him asleep, I went directly to the third floor and was surprised to see Kris in his room.

With an index finger pressed to his lips, he motioned me forward with his other hand.

I stepped toward him as he kept his finger in place, assuring I approached silently. "Watch his eyes," he whispered.

In a deep sleep, Elijah's eyes rolled under their lids. I looked at Kris and shrugged my shoulders. *What's he asking?*

"Watch the flutter."

"Everyone does that," I said, seeing nothing unusual about his REM sleep.

Kris nudged me to the door and into the hallway. "Stand here. Watch." He pointed to Elijah, then turned to Leah.

Too quick to dismiss him, I returned to Elijah's room, and he followed.

With only a glance at the boy, I turned to his drawings, neatly stacked on the dresser.

I drew a deep breath, and exhaled, thankful that Elijah didn't respond to the rustle of pages as I took the entire stack.

Rebecca had been watching me through the windows, and stood in Leah's doorway. "He's gonna flip if his drawings aren't there when he wakes up."

"They'll be there." I smiled, remembering Kathleen's warning. *No John Wayne stuff.*

After stepping through the double-doors at the end of the hallway, I turned to the nearest room and swiped my key. Expecting to enter an office, my jaw dropped when I saw that I was way wrong.

The Board had certainly spared no expense on the Conference Room. Divided into quadrants, each section was painted a different color, and illuminated by a corresponding shade of light. In large, bold letters, the corners were labeled: *Database, ICU, Transport,* and *Operations,* and it was easily the most impressive display of technology I'd ever seen.

The far left was yellow, and labeled, 'Operations'. There, a sizable mainframe served the computer network, and I immediately recognized it as being the brain of Meadowsview.

The far right corner was labeled, 'Transport', and lit by a green spotlight.

In the front right, closest to the door, 'ICU' was painted on the wall, and several monitors displayed live video of each of the intensive care patients. Their vitals scrolled across the bottom of the screen like CNN news. Lit in an eerie shade of maroon, that corner was almost blood red, as though to stress the significance of the decisions made in that quadrant. There, two doctors sipped coffee while discussing details of an upcoming surgery. "It's a Hail Mary," one of them said. "But if it works..."

I stopped in front of Leah's monitor. The view of her room was from a camera mounted in the corner, above her door. It showed her bed, and part of the window to the outside.

Near the back wall, between Operations and Transport, was a large conference table that could easily seat twenty or more. *How appropriate,* I thought. *The King has a round table.*

Halfway through the room I heard the door buzz and turned around. His dreadlocks bounced as he approached. "Are you *crazy*, mon?" Kris said. "That boy will *wig* when he wakes!"

"It's okay. I'll have them back in a few minutes."

"No problem," he smirked. "Do as you will."

— — —

"Kris? Where are you?" Leah shouted as the branches unwound completely and the train advanced. With no choice but to run, she rushed across the bridge, repeating, "Kris! Where are you?" But her shrieks were drowned out by the whistles of the coming locomotive. She looked below, to the large oak tree, where Elijah twirled on the tire swing. Oblivious, he didn't flinch as she yelled, "Elijah!"

Halfway across, she felt the vibrations and knew there was no turning back. Her only chance was the ladder her father had forbidden her and her brother to ever touch.

"Elijaaaaah!" she screamed, running between the tracks, and then looking behind her.

I can't make it! It's too close!

Terrified, Leah chose another option. She stepped to the edge, where she knelt and placed her hands on two wooden planks.

I spread Elijah's drawings across the table. *This is the one she told me about.* Drawn with startling precision, it looked like a photograph of the bridge I'd crossed the day before. Several feet under the distinctive awning, a woman stood staring soberly out, and I saw for myself why Kathleen had contacted me. It *was* Kathleen.

I looked at the next drawing.

"Girl," Rebecca said, frowning and shaking her head. "Your brother's gonna..." *No, not again!* Leah's vitals suddenly spiked, and the nurse, not to make the same mistake as before, pressed the intercom. "Karen, please come quickly."

Horrified, Leah lowered herself over the side of the bridge, letting her legs dangle in the air as she stared at the large metal wheels coming closer.

I have to do it! The train was only a few feet away when she quickly wrapped her palms around the edge, and with all the strength she could marshal, she let her weight fall on her two small hands. Her body swayed high above the riverbed as the entire bridge vibrated mercilessly. "Please, God! Make it go away!"

Rolling from side to side in his bed, Elijah was haunted by a nightmare, and his head bounced uncontrollably up and down on the pillow. His eyes fluttered wildly under their lids as he battled the demons of his sleep. He wanted to reach out to his sister, but he had promised to never again talk-talk, and he could now only watch as she swung helplessly above.

I turned to the next drawing and drew a deep breath. The ability shown in Elijah's work was incomparable, mesmerizing. To have such a gift was amazing, but to have such a gift and be autistic was a miracle.

The leaves on his trees seemed to move in the wind, each uniquely formed to produce the optimal effect of the sunlight he placed in the top left corner. *God, how does he do this?*

Startled by a sudden light over the table, I turned to Dr. Young, who appeared equally surprised to see me.

"Well, good morning, David," he greeted me with groggy eyes, and then stepped down into the conference area, where he poured a large cup of coffee. "I see I'm not the only early bird."

"Actually, I had trouble sleeping," I responded with a short gaze, then turned back to the drawing.

"Working?" he asked as he approached the table.

"Yes, looking at Elijah's drawings."

"Good…good." He stopped a few feet away. "I hear he's quite the artist. By the way, if you're able to, I'd like you to join us for a meeting this evening. We'll be reviewing the Goforth cases."

"Absolutely," I answered, surprised and somewhat flattered by the invitation. "What time?"

"Five o'clock," he said, and took a sip of the coffee.

"Yes, I'll be here."

"Good. Coffee, David?"

"No thanks," I said, with hopes of getting an hour or two more sleep.

Maybe it was the early morning calm or his half-awake condition, but my perception of Dr. Young was somehow changed during our brief conversation. I considered that perhaps I'd been hasty to label him based on our first meeting.

―――――

Kris's tasks had become so routine that he could tell exactly what time it was by which room he was cleaning. He emptied the garbage receptacles, spot-mopped the rooms and, right on schedule, at four-thirty he began mopping the third floor hallway.

He'd observed several other patients as they slept, and none of them showed any resemblance to the way the twins dreamed. The pattern of four counts to the side and three up and down somehow seemed relevant, important.

Karen decided that Leah's condition warranted alerting Dr. Scott, and pressed three digits on the intercom.

A sleepy voice said, "Hello?"

"Sorry to wake you, but Leah's heart rate and BP are

up."

"Again? I'll be right down."

— — —

Leah hung over the gorge, her body weighing heavily on the small fingers that barely kept a hold on the violently shaking planks. "God, make it stop!" she plead. "Make it stop! Or have you left me too?"

Like a rabbit in the talons of a predator in flight, she awaited the mercy of the fall.

Barely clinging to the planks, she started to slip and screamed. For a split second, she considered letting go. *But that's a sin and I won't go to Heaven.* "Krissss," her voice rang through the gorge, and was followed by a drop in the vibrations.

The train passed, and its whistle reverberated through the opposite tunnel.

Leah tried to pull herself up, but managed only a few inches. Her arms fatigued, she stubbornly struggled, but lacked the strength to raise her body any further. Her fall seemed inevitable. Dangling in the ghostly silence, she tried merely to sustain her hold. *But I'm not ready!*

When a finger was suddenly pierced by a large splinter, Leah pulled her hand away, releasing part of her already unstable hold on the bridge. And in a fraction of an instant, she began to fall, but didn't. Two hands took hold of her arm and lifted her back onto the bridge.

———

His pulse was still racing when Elijah awakened from his nightmare. Rolling to his side, his eyes adjusted to the light from the hallway, as his right hand moved toward his head, where his fingers wavered up and down.

Greeted with puzzled expressions from both Rebecca and Karen, Kathleen entered Leah's room, looking first at the patient and then the monitors.

"They dropped," Karen reported. "Just all of the sudden her rates dropped to normal."

"That was weird," Rebecca added.

Half asleep, Kathleen placed Leah's wrist between her fingers. She compared the girl's pulse with the digital readout of the monitor, which hung over a corner of the bed—the indisputable judge of her condition. But Kathleen turned away from the perpetually beeping machinery, to the girl whose innocence and loss of hope could never be adequately measured with complex equipment. *What was she... What was she trying to tell me? God.* She stared languidly into Leah's face.

Rebecca broke the silence. "Oh, Dr. Weston was in Elijah's room and has his drawings."

"What!" Kathleen and Karen responded in chorus.

Suddenly wide awake, "Where is he?" Kathleen asked, aware of the potential results.

"He went through the hall doors," the nurse pointed.

Hurrying from the room, Kathleen turned toward the double-doors, but it was too late. Looking through his window, she saw Elijah sitting at the edge of his bed, rocking frantically back and forth. His hands twitched nervously near his face and his distant gaze was fixed on the spot where his drawings *should* have been. The petrified look on the child's face froze her, as Kris looked down the hallway and could see by Kathleen's expression that Elijah had awakened. Moving his bucket to an empty room, he began walking toward her, and they exchanged an uneasy stare, as though neither knew who should go in first.

Kathleen placed her hand on the doorknob. "Get the drawings," she demanded.

Hesitant, she drew a deep breath before opening the door. "Elijah…" she whispered. "Elijah, your drawings will be right here." She tried to comfort him, but knew that he was close to a full-blown eruption. *Damn it, David!*

I managed to see one more of Elijah's drawings before the genial chat with Dr. Young was interrupted by the door's buzz. Striding across the room, Kris was direct. "Elijah's awake," he blurted. "And he wants his drawings."

After a quick glance at an apparently unaffected Dr. Young, who continued sipping his coffee, I immediately placed the two stacks together and tried to hand them to the Jamaican. Quick to decline the offer, he responded with a grin. "I'm not taking them back… you are."

Dr. Young appeared somewhat amused by the declaration, and smiled as I headed toward the hallway with the contraband.

"Good luck, mon," Kris smirked as I left.

"Yeah, thanks a lot."

God what have I done? Elijah's anguished eyes

sobered me to the reality that I'd made another big mistake. *Damn it, David!*

— — —

Leah stood on the tracks with her arms wrapped in a stranglehold around him. Stepping back, she shot the question at Kris with a piercing glare. "Why did you leave me?"

Dropping to one knee, he calmly answered. "I didn't leave you, I waited for you."

Perplexed, the twelve-year-old asked, "But what does that mean? I turned around and you were gone."

Without answering, he looked to each tunnel. "Which way?" he asked.

She stared below, to the dry riverbed lined with smooth rocks of various shapes and sizes. She then looked to her brother, clearly unaware of the horror from which she had narrowly escaped. "Why can't he hear me? I yelled for him, I..." She stopped mid-sentence, remembering what she had told him the day before she shut down...

"Our talk-talk's a sin Elijah. We can't do it anymore. We have to stop." She remembered his confused expression and last silent plea.

But I won't tell anybody...

"It's still a sin, Elijah, and God will know."

"Okay, but..." he spoke aloud, wanting to persuade her, but aware of her stubbornness.

"But nothing!" She rarely raised her voice to him and continued in a lower tone. "Maybe if we're really good they'll come and take us home." Although she tried to appear hopeful, her mind was littered with guilt, doubt, and recurring memories—the kind that should never burden the thoughts of an innocent child.

The next morning Leah failed to awaken, but despite his anguish, Elijah kept his vow not to talk-talk. Promises and secrets between them were sacred—and there were many of both.

The whistle faintly echoed through the far tunnel, as she looked first there and then to cavern from which they came. "I don't think I should choose this time." She stared at her twin silently swinging in the distance. "You choose."

———

Through his window, I saw Kathleen, frantically responding to Elijah's shrieks. Unsure of what to do, she stood behind him, her hand wavering as though she wanted to comfort him, but feared touching him would only add fuel to the fire.

Stepping inside, I showed him the stack. But he was beyond pissed off, and the sight of me holding his cherished drawings only made things worse. When one fell to the floor, his screams grew louder.

"Dr. Feldman's on her way." She looked at me with hurt, and disbelief that I'd been so reckless.

While I carefully placed the pages on the exact same spot where they were before, the door opened and Annie stepped inside.

"Elijah," she calmly whispered.

Still screaming, he looked up.

Kathleen gladly stepped aside, respectful of Annie, who maintained eye contact with him as she crossed the room and spoke in an authoritative, but assuring, voice. "Elijah, it's okay… where's your box?"

For a moment his wail stopped, and he glanced toward her with red, swollen eyes. Glaring at me, he pointed a brutally unsteady index finger, as though reporting that I was the reason for this ordeal. And I was.

"David, perhaps you could give us a moment." I appreciated her non-accusatory tone as Annie evicted me from the room.

"David, wait," Kathleen said from behind me as I approached the elevator. Her expression was written with the question I knew was coming. "What was that all about?"

Shrugging, I thought about it. Surely, I could come up with some reasonable answer. Finally, I looked her straight in the eyes and gave the best reply I could manage. "Elijah's the key to Leah."

"I already know that. But why did you have to sneak his drawings, and at this time of day?"

"I don't know." I struggled for words. "I just... I just thought I should look at them."

"I can understand that. But why now?" With a hand on my shoulder, she forced me to look her in the eyes. "Couldn't it have waited til the morning? Seriously?"

"I'm sorry," I said. "I didn't think he would wake up."

"Let's get our coats. We're taking a walk."

Here it comes—when*ever we take a walk she has something on her mind. And I know what that something is...*

Twilight in the eastern sky barely lit the path we followed. Exhaled into the bitter New England air, our frosty breaths were out of synch and quickly swept away by the morning breeze.

Looking behind us, all of the third floor windows were lit, as daybreak silhouetted Meadowsview, casting a rustic orange tone over the building.

Don't let it be now, I thought, but knew that this was the moment I'd been dreading.

"What happened?" she wasted no time asking.

Though I knew very well what she was talking about, I avoided the topic.

"I don't know. I couldn't sleep and..."

"No. That's not what I mean," she was quick to interrupt. With a look that confirmed that this *was* the moment, she folded her arms in front of her. "Why haven't you been taking my calls?"

"I've been completely overwhelmed lately."

"What? Too overwhelmed to answer a call? You're gonna have to do way better than that. I can't believe you." She hastened the pace, not about to settle for my half-assed reply. "We used to talk everyday, even after I moved here. I just don't get how I became so irrelevant to you."

"You know that's not true." I thought briefly about my reflection in the mirror only days before, then glanced at my left wrist. *Jesus, if she only knew.* "You mean more to me than you realize." It was a fact. In contrast to everything else in my life—my career, drinking, delusions of Lani—Kathleen helped to stay me reasonably grounded. Feeling the weight of her stare, I faced her.

"What happened on the island, David?" Bluntly stating it—as if she'd narrowed it down, and was certain that it was when I changed—she stepped in front of me.

"Nothing. Nothing happened. Okay?"

"You are *not* gonna try to hand me that!" Angry, she continued. "I know you too well, so don't insult me by saying 'nothing' happened. Maybe you caught some tropical disease, or maybe you were tortured by a tribe of pygmies!" Laughing, she went on. There was no stopping her now, she was on a roll. "Wait! I've got it! You were hexed by a witch doctor, who turned you into a real prick."

"Wait. Did you just call me a prick?" I couldn't help but laugh. "Okay. Maybe I deserve that."

"Oh, you deserve at *least* that much. I mean, really? You avoid me for more than a year, and think it's alright?"

"Aren't pygmies only in Africa?"

Unamused, she started walking again, faster than before. And when we reached the northwest corner of the meadow, several crows called out.

— — —

"Sometimes you have to go back to move forward." Kris clutched Leah's hand as they began through the tunnel from which they came.

"There are some things I'll *nevah* go back to." She began leading him at a faster pace.

"Like what?"

She didn't answer. With her gaze fixed on the

cylinder's entry, several things came to mind, but she blocked them out, and he didn't ask again.

As the evening light faded, they stepped once more into the clearing where the path split. Nervously, she stared at the tall evergreens lining the way to the fortress.

"Leah, come. Come rest." It was the voice of the girl that had called to her before.

"Who is she?" she asked Kris.

"Maybe someone you can trust," he answered. "A friend."

"I trusted *you*," she said. "But you let me go the wrong way."

"I didn't let you. *You* decided the way. The choices here are yours," he added.

"Leah," the girl repeated. "Come."

"So, which way?" he asked. "Which way do you choose?"

She faced the evergreens, and took the trail that led to hospice.

Annie didn't see Elijah the way most people did, as a burden or liability. She was instead awed by his concentration and ability to draw with such exactness. But despite the many hours she'd observed him, only twice had she felt as if she had any true insight into his mindwork. Noting his skills, and lack thereof, she'd reached several conclusions—the most blatant being the fact that he was talented beyond measure. She wondered how he could be so gifted, yet so detached.

"Why don't you draw for us?" She placed a sheet of

white paper on the desk in front of him, causing him to rock slower. He looked at the empty page, and like a photograph in a tray of developer, the image began to appear in his mind.

Twenty-six minutes after he awakened, Elijah sat with silent intensity that chilled her spine. He brandished the pencil while staring at Annie with a severity that stated, "I'll forgive, but not forget." David's intrusion would not be overlooked.

With his pencil clenched tightly between his fingers, there were no complications—only truths, lies and the possessed passion with which he drew his pictures. To many, his ability seemed far outweighed by his struggles, but when Elijah drew, it was with celestial guidance. Leah, a pencil, and blank pages, these were the only anchors in his ocean of introspection. The sanctity and curse of a life spent tethering this world—close enough to examine it, but separate, isolated. Still, he saw everything—the subtle changes of every moment, the shadows as they grew longer and faded away, hate, disgust, deception, contempt, cruelty—everything was taken inside, where he was unable to sort it out. He was God's child, given the gift of perception, but along with it, an inability to grasp the brutal nature of man. And Meadowsview was a scary place, another change, as he felt like a marble in a box, rolling from corner to corner. Confused, he wondered why his mother hadn't come for them, and why he was in a hospital room across the hall from his twin.

He recalled the scent of her hair as she held him to her chest and whispered, "You're God's child, a gift!" And it was Naomi who had taught him and Leah to talk-talk. "Close your eyes," she said. "Listen to the wind." Naomi's hair was straight and long, and it blew in the wind like the mane of a black stallion. Tsa la ghi, she was Cherokee, and it was easy to see that the twins were her blood. "Listen to your heart, and when you hear it beating, listen to the blood flow through your veins."

Mommy taught us how, so how can it be a sin? His mind reeling from loneliness and stress, he closed his eyes and sent the question with the intensity of a bolt of lightning. W*hy's it a sin? Why? Why's it a sin?*

— — —

Caught off guard, Leah stopped and leaned against the trunk of a tall pine. Eyes opened wide, *No Elijah...* she thought. But it was too late.

It's not a sin, he shouted, *it's not!*

Though she'd tried desperately to reach him only moments before then, she knew he would only try to convince her to return. Covering her ears, she began running up the trail.

It's not a sin! His words were inescapable. *Why's it a sin?*

No, Elijah!

Why's it a sin?

He was relentless, and so she closed her eyes then blasted the thought. *Because we're wicked! We're evil!*

Gripping his pencil, he snapped it, drawing Annie's attention. She noticed the veins in his temples as he threw it across the room.

We're not evil! We're not wicked!

"Have you ever been this far?" I asked when we came to the gravel road.

"No, I always stayed closer to the hospital."

"Close to home, huh?" I grinned.

"Don't push it," she replied, "you're already on thin ice." She reminded me that she wasn't accepting my reticent response to her question about the island.

When we got closer, I started to mention the bridge, but after only a few more steps, it was in plain sight.

Kathleen stood paralyzed. "Oh my God..." Her stare was fixed on the arched entry. "David?" She needed answers, but it wasn't that simple. No. There was no clear explanation, and trying to make sense of it was futile.

Fractal waves. Thought transference. I considered giving her one of my standard analogies, but couldn't. Not this time, when she was frightened, confused, and turning to me for resolve.

I recalled the shy southern girl who sat in the back of the lecture hall. Always twisting her hair, she seemed out of her element and rarely spoke. It took me more than two months to work up the nerve to start a conversation. And once I did, it took less than two minutes to realize that she was special. Kathleen was unlike anyone I'd ever known.

Back then, neither of us knew our place in the world, and we were opposite in nearly every way. But we seemed to understand each other, and became the best of friends.

Now, reunited by incomparable circumstances, her green eyes plead for reason.

"Maybe you're more involved than you know," I said.

"What?"

"Did he draw your dream, or did you dream of his drawing?" Was she a sender, a receiver, a relay? Regardless, there was no doubt that she was a part of the equation.

It's waiting. At first, it was no louder than the rustle of the leaves in the wind. Then she repeated, *It's waiting.* Louder, closer, Lani sounded like she was only a few steps away, but was nowhere in sight.

Not now, I thought. *Please, not now. I tried to ignore her, but couldn't.*

"David? Are you okay?"

"Yes," I answered. "Yeah, I'm fine." My face was flush, and hands trembled.

The bridge, Lani repeated.

"What bridge?" I pointed at Goforth's Crossing. *"This* bridge?"

"What? What's going on?" Kathleen asked.

"Didn't you hear that?" I faced her.

"Hear what?"

The train bridge.

"That—that voice." I looked into the dense woods on both sides.

"This isn't funny," she said. "I'm already mortified, and you're making *jokes?"*

"No," I answered. "No. Maybe it's just the wind."

But it wasn't the wind. I felt Lani's presence every

step of the way back to Meadowsview.

Chapter 8 – Assemblies

The congregation was unusually quiet, as many were wondering how Reverend Goforth would respond to Naomi's death. A few of his most devout followers openly wept while he stared distantly through the west window.

He then walked slowly to the pedestal, looking every bit the part of the grieving husband. But it wasn't grief that moved him. Though his vulnerable appearance played well with the audience, he was driven by other motives.

"Examine me," Jacob began the sermon, and the words echoed through the church. "Examine me," he repeated, holding the Book above his head. "The twenty-sixth Psalms says... "

Everyone knew that when the reverend named a chapter, they were expected to read along—or just pretend to. And while the worshipers turned to the Book of Psalms, he sipped his water and placed the glass on the pulpit.

His steel gray eyes were unnerving as Jacob's voice rang through the walls. "Examine me, O Lord, for I have walked with integrity."

The congregation, disheartened by poverty and hardship, believed in his promises of eternity. They were the people of the hills, and he was their spiritual leader, the deliverer of hope. And now, in his time of greatest sorrow, his mere presence was proof of his faith in God.

Through the window, he saw a hawk circling a nearby canyon. Predator. Prey. Jacob had been both, and wished at that moment that he too could fly away.

"We live in troubled times." He slowly paced the floor. "We live in times of hunger, war, violence, and moral decline." He paused, looking again to the window. "But in Psalms, David tells the Lord he shall not slip. Test me! Examine me, God! For you will find I have walked in Your truth!"

"Amen," several voices responded. The sinners and righteous, struggling workers and mothers, black, white, young and old, all knew that the good reverend was only warming up. The walls would soon rattle with the Word of God ringing through the aisles.

At the pulpit, he clutched his Bible firmly in his right hand. "The time is upon all good Christians to ask God to examine them." He looked into the eyes of the faithful.

With raised hands, they answered "Amen" and "Halleluiah!"

"You!" Jacob admonished a man at the back of the

church. "Brother James." All eyes turned to the teenager bearing a sheepish grin. "Did you enjoy that beer and cigarette last Sunday at the pool hall?"

"James!" his mother chastised.

"Sin is everywhere," Jacob continued, as his flock turned back, each with their own transgressions.

"Temptation breeds quickly in our world, but He will be merciful only to those who have washed their hands of ignorance. Only they will sit at the Lord's Altar and dwell in the House of God!" The packed church sat watching as he pounded his chest. "Sin is here!" And yes, Jacob knew sin well.

With her arms folded in front of her, Kathleen walked a few steps ahead of me. Surely thinking of the bridge, she said nothing as we returned to the hospital.

At a hallway corner, I literally bumped into Dr. Feldman. "I'm so sorry." I laughed, embarrassed for having nearly knocked her down.

"I was actually hoping to bump into you, David, but maybe not quite like this," she smiled. "If you've got a moment, would you mind helping me move my desk?"

"No, of course not," I answered, curious about her request.

"Look, I have patients to see, so I'll catch up with you later. And don't forget about the meeting tonight." Kathleen waited for the elevator as Annie led me to her office.

"I guess I should've taken these things off already." She began removing stationary and nick-knacks from the broad desktop. "You'll have to excuse me for not being ready." She motioned to a comfortable leather sofa. "Won't you have a seat, David? This won't take long."

As I sat down, I found it interesting that she chose me to help her with the task, especially when there were any number of others she could have asked.

"So tell me a little about yourself," she casually said, confirming that the desk wasn't really why I was there. "Tell me about your childhood," she added with surprising directness.

"Ohhhh, okay," I grinned, but my chest tightened. "We can call this our 'therapy for moving furniture deal'."

"Or you could just call it a favor to me." She stared over the rim of her glasses. "Besides, this shouldn't take very long." She placed a neon green stapler in the box.

Although I was in need of counseling, the prospect of disclosing bits and pieces of my life was nerve-racking, especially to someone as highly trained and perceptive as Annie. I wondered if Kathleen had put her up to it.

"Like what?" I finally replied.

"Just whatever comes to mind—riding your bike, sports, something from your past that moved you."

Put on the spot, several thoughts crossed my mind, but I chose instead to give a token response.

"Well, my brother and I used to ride our bikes on the trails near the creek."

"I'm sure those are great memories."

"Yeah, we wiped out a few times, and pedaled home pretty scratched-up, but we always seemed to go back."

Seeing that I wasn't offering anything more than

minimal appeasement, "Surely there's something else?" she said. "Something that left an impression. Something that contributed to who you are."

I thought back, then remembered when I was eleven. "I was in the fifth grade," I said. "And I found a nest with speckled blue eggs."

"Now *that's* a memory, isn't it? Please, go on..."

"So I checked on them everyday, pretending to be an archaeologist who found raptor eggs," I smiled. "I even carried a compass and pocket knife."

"So you had a good imagination?"

"I guess... Actually, yes, I had a great imagination. I could always entertain myself."

"And what were you like then?"

"Quiet. Shy."

She discreetly sat in her chair. "Friends? Did you have any?"

"A few," I answered. "But I was closer to John than anyone else."

"Your brother?"

"Yeah. I spent my time with him, or alone. Mostly alone."

"Give me one word that describes how you felt back then."

"Compliant." It was the first word that came to mind. "My dad was... old school."

"Did he beat you?" she asked with no hesitation, as if she already knew the answer.

"On occasion," I answered. "Report card days were especially brutal."

"He beat you for bad grades?"

"No. My brothers."

"I see," she said. "And so you were torn between guilt and relief. And what did your mother do?"

"What *could* she do?" I recalled her attempts to get him to stop. "Once he got going, there was no stopping him. So much for report card day, huh?"

"Yes. So tell me more about the nest."

"Well," I said, glad to be back on the other topic. "It was in a grove beyond our property line, in a Brazilian Pepper tree.

"Two mockingbirds called out from another tree, and I knew it was their nest, but that didn't stop me. No. It was my secret discovery, and I checked every day, hoping to find baby birds with mouths opened wide.

"One day, I decided to touch them...

"Standing on a sturdy branch, I reached into the nest, while the angry birds flew over me. Shrieking, diving, they were determined to drive me away from the grove.

"After jumping from a lower branch, I pulled the hood of my jacket over my head, but they continued the assault until I'd disappeared through our back door.

"The next day I returned, but stopped several steps away from the grove. Gray and black feathers were scattered across the trail, and led to the remains of a dead bird—the victim of a cat. A few steps further, I stood over the other dead mockingbird.

"Expecting to find the nest empty, I climbed the tree faster than ever, and with a sudden sense of purpose, I adopted the three speckled eggs.

"'David, come and eat,' my older brother called from our house.

"I should bury them, I thought, as I came to the ant-ridden vestiges. Admiring the ferocity with which they tried to protect their unborn, I dug a shallow hole beside a cactus, then dropped the songbirds in it.

"Filled with a mix of sorrow and empowerment, it was a milestone, landmark, a coming of age. Having laid claim to the orphaned eggs, it was now my responsibility to see if I could make them hatch. *I'll feed them insects, worms, whatever birds eat. And I'll cover the eggs tomorrow.*"

Why this memory? Why now?

She'd been listening intently, her elbows now on the desk, and chin in her hands, as I considered the gravity of the things I'd told her.

"And what happened to your eggs, David?"

"Well. Two of them never hatched."

"And the third egg?" she finally asked.

Sometimes we summon memories, while others just come—inalterable threads in the cloth of our lives, the substance of that which has colored, or tainted us in some way.

"Alright, I think we're ready," she said, sensing my anxiety, and knowing I'd gone as far as I would with my account of the nest. "I just want to move it over a little." She pointed to a window. "So the light doesn't hit me in the eyes."

The effort took all of one minute, and I returned to my room, thinking about my dad, and the nest I hid under my bed.

Leah's file was a welcome diversion. There had to be

something in the pages that would lead in the right direction, and I spent a good part of the day looking for it. But despite the hours I spent reviewing the case, I felt completely unprepared as I entered the Conference Room.

The staff greeted me with polite smiles, as I adjusted my tie before taking a seat.

"Glad you could join us," Dr. Young courteously nodded to my side of the table. "First, let me introduce Dr. Weston, researcher, and adviser for the Goforth case."

Looking around the table, I smiled as The King continued. "Dr. Weston is a guest of our psychology department. Would you like to say a few words?" He motioned in my direction with one hand.

"Umm, sure," I responded, not expecting to address the group. "First of all, please call me David."

"Wait," a voice interrupted. It was Dr. Svelgaard. "David Weston, the writer of dreams?"

"Yes," I replied, "the writer of dreams."

"I've heard of your research." He looked at me like a cat hovering over a cornered mouse. "And what do you *really* hope to find?"

"I'd like to find out several things, Jon."

"It's Doctor," he replied. "The title I prefer, if that's okay, David."

"Sure. Okay, Doctor Jon," I said, to which he merely grinned.

"Like what? I mean, what do you hope to contribute to this? What kind of enlightenment can you provide us with?"

"I don't know if I can enlighten you at all, Doctor," I

shot back. "But maybe I can help discover why Leah's still unconscious."

Seeing the direction of our exchange, "David, we're *all* trying to make that determination," Kathleen said, while Dr. Svelgaard, despite his own provocation, seemed noticeably affronted by my response.

"It just seems to me that there's no medical reason for her coma." To Kathleen's dismay, I continued. "So how can you expect medicine and doctors to bring her back? Medicine won't wake her up. External devices won't wake her up. We have to dig into her subconscious."

Jon, of course, disagreed. "We don't know that, Doctor," he said mockingly, questioning my credentials to even discuss the matter. "And how do you propose we 'dig in'?"

The room was silent, and judging by their expressions it seemed that Jon wasn't the only one curious about my practices.

"Well, let's back up for a minute. Did she show indications of brain trauma?" I looked directly at him.

"No," he responded.

"No," I parroted, and pointedly continued. "Is she diabetic, or is there evidence of any other medical reason for her state?"

Smirking back, "None that we know, yet," he answered.

"And her brainwaves are intact?" Looking at the tabletop, I then glanced into several faces which were uncomfortably quiet. "Yes, her mind is stimulated," I answered for him.

"We're aware of that. But what exactly is it that you

hope to achieve?"

Dr. Young took over. "Perhaps now would be a good time to hear the agenda." He turned to his right.

"First topic, Elijah Goforth," his secretary responded.

Annie, who was seated directly across from me, then asked, "Is there any reason we can't move Elijah to another floor?"

"For what purpose?" Dr. Young questioned.

"I believe he'd do much better in a more suitable atmosphere. The activity of the third floor seems less likely to keep him calm." One-by-one she turned to the agreeing nods of several others, but it was understood that the King, under advisement of his worthy knights, would ultimately make the decision.

"Yes, I see your point, but where would we move him?" He looked at Annie, knowing she must have already thought of a place.

She answered directly, "Across from my office are two rooms that haven't been used for a while. We could easily convert one into his room, and the other into a station for a member of the nursing staff."

"Are there any arguments against moving Elijah to the first floor?" Dr. Young looked completely around the table, into the faces of what I had counted to be twelve people.

A smirk came from beside me. "You mean that room where we keep our golf clubs?"

"Well, it looks like you boys will have to find another place for your toys," Annie stared over the rim of her glasses.

"Yes," Dr. Young grinned in agreement, and with

complete confidence asked, "Dr. Feldman, would you mind organizing the remodel with the maintenance department?"

"Not at all," she politely answered. There was clearly camaraderie between them based on mutual respect.

With the relocation approved, Dr. Young asked the group, "Any additional thoughts about Elijah?"

"Photocopies of his work would be nice." I faced him, and then Annie, who asserted her approval.

"Yes, that's a great idea." She looked at the head of the table, who again gave his stamp of approval.

"Yes, well, whatever you think you need." Dr. Young glanced around for other suggestions, and finally back at me.

Not wanting to miss an opportunity, I started to make another request. "We all know of Elijah's talent." A few nodded as I continued assuredly. "His drawings are his only real contact with this world."

"But is that fact or opinion?" Dr. Svelgaard chimed in again, looking first at me, then at Annie, who quickly responded.

"I think David's very much on the right track."

The entire staff, including the neurosurgeon, respected Dr. Feldman, and I was glad she'd spoken on my part.

She went on. "However, Elijah is grounded mostly by his sister. Leah is his real link, his balance." She looked confidently around the table, and began her assessment of the Goforth Situation. "He's alone and confused. To tell you the truth, I'm surprised he's held it together as well as he has. But he knows she's alive, and *that's* his focus."

Nobody responded. She'd spent many hours with him, and her statements were considered to be stone cold facts.

"And David's right," she added, "his drawings deserve attention."

"I'm confused." Jon faced Ian. "Are we here to discuss a girl in a coma, or her brother's drawings?" In typical Svelgaard style, he derailed any hope of us having a reasonable exchange. He spun in his chair, directing the statement at me, "Photographs of his drawings won't help his sister."

Before responding, I glanced at Kathleen, who had started twisting her hair. Her deer-in-the-headlights expression was laughable. *Stay cool. Exercise restraint.* I'd seen that look many times before. But he'd made it personal, and she knew me better than to think I wouldn't respond.

My initial thought was *Fuck you, Jon,* but I drew a few deep breaths and kept my composure—the last thing I wanted to do was embarrass Kathleen.

"I'd like to look at his drawings," I calmly stated. "Or will that somehow interfere with what you're doing that's working so well?"

"We have *two* cases here," he answered. "You're trying to make them into one."

"I'm exploring possibilities that you're incapable of considering."

"If you mean I'm incapable of considering Jung's theories, you're right." In a single sentence, he both discredited and dismissed my research.

"Jon," Annie interrupted. "David's a guest of my

department, and I expect him to be treated as such."

"No, it's okay," I said, facing him. "It's just a shame that someone with your skills can know so little about the subconscious."

Dr. Young, who had been quietly enjoying our exchange, finally spoke. "Yes. Well, we seem to have gotten off topic. Copies of Elijah's work will be made. But—and I think we're all curious about this—what will you do with them?"

"Look for consistencies, and contrasts. I'll try to create a root index of relative words and symbols."

"Relative words?" Svelgaard mocked. "Relative to what?"

At this point, I knew that arguing with him was futile.

"Relative to his twin," I answered. "Try to keep up, Jon."

"Dr. Feldman, what can you tell us about Elijah?" The King was ready to move forward.

Annie placed both hands on the table. "He's complex," she said, as several others leaned back in their chairs, ready to be taken into the mind of Elijah Goforth.

— — —

After they rounded a hairpin corner, the fortress was suddenly in plain sight. Covered with knee-high blades of bluish grass, the trail had been been rarely traveled, causing Leah to hesitate.

"Not many people come here," she said.

"Or maybe they come another way," Kris responded.

Large stones covered with fluorescent purple moss formed a path that led around the dark side of the fortress. And above them, the familiar voice of the other girl was clear and assuring. "Come Leah," she beckoned. "Come rest on silken sheets."

"His drawings aren't just pretty pictures." Annie looked around the table. "His work is how he copes with his limitations. Basically, it's how he deals with circumstances he has no way of changing." With everyone's attention, she went on. "As with most autistic children, routine is important, but his has been destroyed. There's no sense of normalcy, so he fills the hours drawing—it's probably the only thing that keeps him from having more meltdowns."

Jon tried again to insert his two cents, but Annie wasn't finished.

"We have unusual conditions here which require our immediate attention."

"What do you need?" Dr. Young asked.

"A connection," she answered. "I suggest we allow Dr. Weston to perform his test, and see what he comes up with."

Only the King was prepared for what came next.

Dressed in slacks, a wrinkled white shirt, and a tie, Kris came directly to the table and took a seat. "Sorry I'm late. I overslept," he grinned.

"That's quite alright," Ian replied. "Everyone else managed to make it on time, but, by all means, have a seat. We're all here at your leisure. Would anyone care to fill our latecomer in on what he's missed during... " he looked at his Rolex, "the last twenty-five minutes?"

"I'm sorry, Sir. I sleep days, work nights." Kris defended himself by merely stating facts. It was obvious that he'd been invited to the meeting, and I wondered why. Then it dawned on me that Annie wasn't the only one who had spent time with the twins.

"Elijah Goforth is our topic," Dr. Young looked at Kris, presenting him with a chance to speak.

"Elijah," Kris paused, looking into the faces of those wondering why the hell the custodian was there. "He knows her dreams." Noticeably uncomfortable, he leaned over the table, and hesitantly continued. "And he wants to change them," he added with a sober, certain stare.

"That's absurd!" Everyone turned immediately to Dr. Svelgaard, and I couldn't help but laugh, drawing his glare. "And you of course share this line of thought?" This time he shot daggers, and, having had enough of his arrogance, I decided to turn the tables.

"And Dr. Svelgaard, you believe the case warrants no paranormal research?"

"I believe a little girl is in a coma, and like I said before, we have two separate cases here. To try to make them into one is a waste of time."

"Or perhaps you're merely incapable of seeing anything in other than academic terms. I bet you have an explanation for everything, even those you don't understand."

"Maybe you can beat each other up another time," Kris asserted. "What about the flutter?" He faced me, seeking support.

"Yes, the flutter…" I had no idea what he was talking about.

He sat grinning for a moment, disappointed that I didn't say anything. Admirably, he didn't give up.

"A lot of help you are," he smirked and continued. "The twins at night, when they sleep... " With all eyes captive, he raised his hands and made identical motions with his index fingers.

Then, I remembered. "Watch the flutter," he'd said before I took the drawings. He was trying to show me Elijah's eye movement.

Validation came from the overnight Head Nurse. "That's true," Karen said. "When they're sleeping, the twins are almost impossible to tell apart."

"Okay, so we all know they look alike." Jon was agitated by the possibility of anything other than a clinical diagnosis.

"Excuse me, but I wasn't finished." Turning to Dr. Young, she continued. "One night I stood between their rooms and watched them." Her frank expression drew looks of anticipation. "I think Kris is right, it's almost like they're having the same dream."

"That's ridiculous," the neurosurgeon grinned, not buying what he considered 'psychic mumbo-jumbo.'

"And what about the drawings?" Kris asked. "Dr. Weston's the only one to look at the boy's pictures, and it's all right there in black and white."

"Well, actually I've looked at them too." Annie said, with her trademark grasp of an earpiece. "And haven't you, Kathleen?"

Having told Annie, in confidence, about her dream and Elijah's drawing, Kathleen felt like she'd been thrown under the bus. She looked at Annie with surprise.

"Yes," she hesitantly responded, recalling the chill she felt when she first saw the rendering. "Some of you will question this," she began, knowing that some of the others shared Jon's skepticism. "But I believe that Elijah has... abilities."

"Abilities?" Dr. Young asked.

"Psychic abilities."

A few chuckles immediately followed, the loudest, of course being Dr. Svelgaard. "Are you serious, Ian, you've brought us here for a séance?"

The King scratched his head. "Well, Dr. Scott went to the trouble of calling a medium from California. So what now, David? Do we hold hands and chant? Did you remember the candles?"

"Well, they took my candles at LAX. They even took my voodoo charms."

"Wait. I've got a Ouija Board in my office," Annie said with a straight face.

After a few much needed laughs, Dr. Young asked Kathleen, "What makes you think that? What proof do you have?"

"There is none," Jon wasted no time in answering for her. "Now do you mind if I get back to my patients?" He stood as though the meeting was over.

Thrusting his fist on the table, Dr. Young commanded attention. "Doctor, this meeting has not been adjourned." His leadership was not to be questioned. "Jon, you told me yourself that you feel like you're still at square one, and how time's running short. I know it's unorthodox, but, at Dr. Scott's request, David's here to find answers that have somehow eluded our medical department. And if a séance is what it takes to wake her up, count me in."

"You look here," Kris interrupted, smiling as he put a finger on his temple. "But the twins? The twins are joined here." He pointed to his chest. "You see a forest but not the trees." He faced Jon, and then, in an unexpected nod of encouragement, directed his stare at me. "Maybe your way will find where they meet."

"Well." The King cleared his throat. "Look around this room." Each of us viewed the array of computers and sophisticated equipment. "Meadowsview possesses the most advanced medical technology available." We all listened and wondered where he was going with this. "And now, take a look around this table." He paused for a moment while we traded curious glances. "Some of you are considered to be among the top minds in your field. Annie, your work speaks for itself." He turned to Dr. Svelgaard. "Jon, your research with neurotransmitters has been published in several journals. And Dr. Weston, many consider your theories to be both well founded and well supported." I smiled appreciatively, knowing we weren't called there for a pat on the back. "But we're up against the clock here, and the reason for this meeting is to address one important question." He looked one-by-one into the faces of each person there. "Why is Leah unresponsive to treatment? I feel that a group like this could answer that question." We looked like a team of salesmen who had missed an important monthly quota. "In fact," he went on, "Miss Goforth's Glasgow Coma Score is actually worse than before."

"I believe we should place an ICP monitor," Jon said.

Kathleen responded. "Is that really necessary?"

I didn't know what it was about an ICP, but for some reason she was opposed to it.

The neurosurgeon continued. "You're aware that this is protocol. It should have been placed when she was admitted."

"Is there a valid medical reason for opposing the procedure?" Dr. Young asked.

"I…" She seemed embarrassed. "I know it's a minor procedure, but it just seems so invasive. I mean, they get here and *bam*, we put a nice little hole in their head. Also, it should be noted that Miss Goforth shows absolutely no signs of head injury."

Dr. Young took it from there. "Dr. Scott, it seems like we've had this discussion before."

"I don't know what you mean." Kathleen suddenly looked like a schoolgirl receiving a lecture from the principal.

"It's minor surgery." He looked to Jon for support.

"A bedside procedure."

Without pause, he rendered his decision. "I agree with Dr. Svelgaard, and the tap will be placed tomorrow morning." The King had spoken.

Kathleen faced Jon, who attempted to deter her anxiety. "It's a simple procedure, and we'll have the ability to react sooner in the event her pressure increases."

She offered a placating smile, but everyone knew she wasn't overjoyed.

"We seem to have moved past our initial topic." Dr. Young wasn't quite finished with the discussion about Elijah. Facing me, he caught me off guard. "Have you monitored two dreaming patients at once?" The question could only mean one thing.

"Yes." I answered.

"What does it entail? I guess I'm asking you what you need us to do."

"Their heads should be shaved," I said. "We'll be placing several additional sensors."

"Karen." He looked at the nurse.

"Yes, Doctor. I'll take care of it."

"Tomorrow night. Eight o'clock. Jon, David, Kathleen, Annie, and Rebecca, clear your schedules." Turning to me, "I'll expect a full report Friday morning," he finished.

With that, the wheels were set in motion for a breakdown involving both twins simultaneously.

"Will you need crystals, or anything?" Jon smirked.

"No," I indulged his sarcasm one last time, "my lucky penny should do the trick."

"Dr. Svelgaard, and Dr. Weston, you two will get to work together on this," the King said, leaving no room for question.

"David will be present for the morning procedure, and Jon will assist tomorrow evening. I suggest you both have an early night."

With a sudden respect for Dr. Young, I nodded in agreement. He'd seemed uninvolved in the case, but had recognized the merit in evaluating the twins at the same time. That alone was praiseworthy.

As I exchanged brief stares with the sanctimonious Dr. Svelgaard, all eyes were upon us, waiting for our reactions.

171

Kris finally broke the silence, summing it up with one line. "And you boys try to get along."

Everyone laughed except Jon and me.

Jacob's followers were so loyal that most attended both his Sunday and Wednesday services—as though doubling their chances of going to Heaven. Some were dependent on the church for not only their spiritual well-being, but also the meager fare it provided for their families. The assembly's food bank was all that sustained many of them during the cold West Virginia winters.

His sermons were well-written and delivered with compelling clarity. A rock, he was above reproach, and his flock believed that God Himself spoke through the six-foot-four Reverend. "Examine me!" Like a battle cry, the words echoed through the aisles, to the faithful, who responded with chants and clapping.

Frequently, members of the assembly were overcome with the Spirit and spoke in strange words. Jacob encouraged such acts of devout faith. "Brothers and Sisters, the Book tells us to be eager to speak in Tongues."

Chapter 9 – Lauani

As he prepared Leah for the pressure monitor, Jon sensed my anxiety. "What kinds of music do you like, David?"

"I'm flexible," I answered, as though unaffected by what I was about to see. With her head shaven, Leah looked even more vulnerable than before. "I listen to pretty much everything, except maybe rap or opera."

He then placed a small cylinder into the end of a handheld drill resembling an old coffee grinder, only shiny and stainless. It wasn't until then that I understood Kathleen's point of view.

God. He's drilling into her skull.

Jon continued with complete confidence as I watched, appreciative of his skill, but readily allowing memories of the island to fill my thoughts...

The day I arrived, Reka helped pitch my tent. Always smiling, but quiet and shy, his thoughtful dark eyes reflected the soul of an Old Spirit. The lone member of the village to have been educated in Wellington, great things were expected of the sixteen year old.

Seeing their perplexed, reticent smiles, I gave the children balloons, which they brought to their lips when I raised one to my mouth and began to blow. Before long there were a dozen Polynesian children circling my green tent with splashes of color. "My lahr bal oons." Young eyes filled with joy as they tried to pronounce the words, their laughter blending well with the sound of crashing waves forty or so steps away.

I then noticed a little girl watching from behind a broad palm tree. Curious, she looked at the balloon in my hand, and smiled when I offered it to her.

She came closer and shyly took it from me, then brought it to her mouth.

After she blew it up, I tied it and gave it back to her. With a probing stare, she held it above her head, then darted across the warm white sand.

She was always there during the interviews. The other children watched for a while and then played, but Lani was always there, observing with the same judicious stare of her brother, Matareka.

Several days after my arrival, the evening sky was particularly vibrant, like a photograph that had been digitally enhanced.

Her alert eyes were fixed on mine with an intensity that couldn't be ignored. Reka noticed her gaze too, and seemed shaken, anxious. His translation of an elder's story halted, and all became silent as the shy child emerged from behind the others. The younger children quickly stepped into the eager embrace of their parents, and it was clear that this was an important moment.

Approaching with the flames of the bonfire reflecting in her dark eyes, Lani inched forward, stopping a little more than an arm's reach away.

She extended her right hand, and in it was a small white orchid, which I gratefully accepted.

She then extended her left hand, holding the limp, punctured remains of the balloon I'd given her.

— — —

Although outwardly she appeared unchanged, Leah's subconscious swirled like embers in a whirlpool.

When the bit hit the bone a numbing chill consumed her. "Kris!" her shrill cry echoed through the corridors. "Kris!" she covered her ears and faced him. "That sound, what is it? What is it?"

"I hear only the girl," he answered.

Vibrating, the drill penetrated the darkest recesses of her subconscious.

Screaming, she fell to her knees, overcome by unbearable pain.

A nightmare within a dream, Leah fell further into the catacombs of delirium.

———

"Done." Jon looked up from his task, into the eyes of his assistants, and lastly into mine, as though to say, "Top that." The procedure had taken only a few minutes, but left an indelible impression in my mind.

With the apparatus in place, it was determined that her pressure was normal, and the immediate staff went about their duties.

Having new appreciation for the Swede's abilities, I merely returned his smile with a sober gaze, knowing that Dr. Young's campaign to unite our efforts was only half complete—Jon would be *my* assistant that evening.

While he instructed the others, I turned to Leah.

What pain could have caused this?

Oblivious to the activity of the third floor, I walked directly down the long hallway to the elevator. Alone inside, I leaned against the door and drew deep breaths as my hands shook uncontrollably.

"David," the whisper came from the speaker on the panel.

The light blinked, then the elevator stopped between floors. And like a sudden change of television stations, my reflection in the metallic door became Lani's.

"Don't be afraid, your trials will pass in the crossing." The words from the speaker were muddled and out of synch with her lips, but she stared with a tranquil smile.

It could have been my imagination, I wished it was, but with the fluorescent light striking her jet black hair, she stood before me with inescapable presence.

"What crossing?" I whispered.

"You already know. And your answers are there."

With another flicker of the lights, the elevator again moved, and the channel switched back. My own reflection returned, but somehow it seemed foreign to me, like someone I used to know, but had changed drastically over time.

I wasn't me, I was the embodiment of a slow breakdown. There was no reprieve from my self-punishment. Nowhere was sanctuary, and forgiveness never to be. *The renowned David Weston.* I mocked the image of my eyes swelling with the guilt and shame of the affliction I brought to the island of Lauani.

"David?" I heard my name, but continued through the front doors.

Not to be ignored, "David," Kathleen repeated. "Don't just walk away from me!" She quickly caught up, but as she grabbed my arm I faced her, and could see she was stunned by my appearance.

Looping her arm in mine, she took quick strides to try to keep up with me. We headed down the path, then cut across the large meadow, where cool gusts of wind scattered more signs of impending winter.

Halfway across the meadow I stopped. "Okay. You wanna know what happened on the island?" Having kept it to myself for so long, I decided to tell her. "I brought impressive equipment. I brought technology." I began walking at a less feverish pace, and she tightened her arm's grip around mine. Fully out of view of the hospital we stopped again, and I told my secret. "And I also brought a fucking case of strep throat."

"It's okay," she said, "It's okay..."

"No. It's *not* okay." I looked her in the eyes, and tried to remain somewhat composed, but after over a year of emotional agony it wasn't easy. "When she got sick they put her in a remote hut on the edge of the village. Only her mother stayed with her." I remembered Lani's innocent eyes when I first went to look at her throat. "I contacted the pilot in Auckland, and told him to bring antibiotics, but I was too late."

She wrapped both arms around me. "No," she said and raised a hand to my face, forcing me to look her in the eyes. "It just happened. You can't blame yourself."

But I *did* blame myself.

"Lani died in her sleep, and I left with the pilot after the burial ritual that night."

"You don't have to talk about it, I understand."

"Do you though? I mean, I don't understand it at all. And to make it worse, they still treated me like a guest, even in their grief. But I felt like a thief who'd taken something precious and irreplaceable. I couldn't look them in the eyes."

"It's okay." She looked with swelling eyes, wanting to comfort me, but knowing there was little she could say or do. "It happened. It's not like you planned it."

"It happened. That's what I've told myself over and over. But I can't forget her eyes, and how her brother seemed so lost..."

"So that's it? This is what you've been keeping from everyone? You've never even told your brother. Jesus, David, have you talked to *anybody*?"

"Like who? I mean, nobody can change anything. No one can take it back. I'd never even had strep before that. Hell, I thought it was just a sore throat."

"It's okay," she repeated.

"You wanted to know, and now you do. They put her body on a raft, and surrounded her with twigs and leaves. And I remember it like it was yesterday."

"God..." Clenching both sleeves of my shirt, she placed her head on my shoulder.

"They threw torches on her and pushed her out into the lagoon." I drew a deep breath, allowing the tears I'd suppressed for much too long, to finally fall. "Then they chanted... prayed for the Gods to take her."

Chapter 10 – Jacob

After a rain, the hills of West Virginia were filled with the scent of chimneys and wet musky leaves. Jacob drove down the narrow country road, his mind consumed with memories of his childhood and Joseph's cold neglect.

He recalled an attempt to gain his father's notice.

"Look daddy! I'm swinging!" Jacob was six years old and swung as high as he could on the large Vermont estate.

Joseph Goforth merely glanced at his son and continued to admonish his groundskeepers for poor performance.

"Daddy, I'm swinging! See? I'm swinging!" He again plead for acknowledgment, but what he received was much different. His father approached, and as Jacob smiled, thinking he was coming to play, held a firm hand out and pushed him off.

He continued driving on the winding road between humble dwellings, where rusted trucks and junk lined many of the yards. The howl of nearby dogs was the only sound, except for those in his unrelenting memories.

"Jacob, come here," his stepmother said while Joseph was away on one of his frequent business trips. "Mix me a drink," she commanded. He was only ten then, but mixed a perfect Martini. "Now rub my feet." She personified the unfulfilled housewife, having entered into a loveless marriage solely for the wealth that Joseph, seventeen years older than her, provided. But where Joseph was neglectful, she was quite attentive, demanding he then massage her neck and shoulders.

The wet pavement reflected the dark sky as Jacob clenched the wheel tighter.

Robbed of a youth and stripped of his innocence, he tried to fight the bitter memories, but couldn't. Even with his children taken away, and Naomi, his angel, buried in a nearby cemetery, thoughts of childhood clouded his mind. Reaching beside him, he grasped his well-worn Bible—the only thing that had never failed him. Someday Joseph would kneel at his feet and beg forgiveness. *Someday,* he thought. *Someday he'll understand what he did, and pay for it.*

Oblivious to his own menacing mindwork, he pounded the steering wheel. Angry, vengeful, *God's will be done,* he thought, but his thoughts lacked guilt and any measure of humility.

Without conscience, Jacob viewed himself as an instrument for good, chosen by God to lead the less fortunate. To him, his actions were justified—condoned by his tragic past. But in trying to become the perfect preacher, he had lost his way and instead become the perfect beast.

Chapter 11 – Kathleen

Neither of us knew what to say.

Clinging tightly to my side, she looked at me frequently, but Kathleen's face was written with the uncertainty of how, or even *if* to continue our talk.

We took a small trail heading west, until it disappeared in dense undergrowth. When she kept going, my curiosity began to mount. *Where's she taking me?* We stepped over fallen branches and leaves, then came to a small clearing.

Pointing to an old shed. "This is where I always come to get away for awhile," she said, looking at me with the same expression she had in the photograph, but this time I recognized it.

Reaching into her smock, she removed a key to the padlock that kept her retreat private. Turning the knob, "I discovered this place one morning when a patient died after one of those 'routine' procedures Jon was talking about." She tried pushing the door open, but the old abandoned tool shed was in disrepair, and it didn't budge. "It's sticking," she mumbled and tried again without luck.

"Why don't you just have the gardeners or someone fix it up for you?"

Looking over her shoulder, "That would take all the fun out of it. Besides, I really don't think they even know it's here, and I kinda like it that way." She kicked the bottom of the door, which then flew open.

Walking across the creaky floor, she struck a match and lit an oil lamp.

Photographs were taped on one wall—birds, leaves, squirrels, she was a natural.

"Yours, huh?" I smiled at a picture of a field mouse peeking his head curiously over a fallen branch.

"Yeah," she answered. "You know how I always wanted to be Ansel Adams."

"Yep, and I always thought you missed your calling." I looked at her photos, then turned behind me. Near the door, four shelves were covered with menageries and trinkets she'd smuggled in the pockets of her smock.

A rocking chair draped with a colorful afghan was in one corner, near the north facing window, and beside it, a wooden table held a second lamp, which she also lit.

"Oh," she said, reaching for a small ceramic heater. "I know you Cali boys don't like the cold." Turning it on, she smiled. "Wouldn't want ya to freeze to death."

Nervous, I wasn't sure how I felt about what I'd told her. On one hand, there was a sense of relief, but on the other I was shameful.

I looked at her trinkets—porcelain fairies and woodland animals. She'd filled the room with cheerful things that allowed her to escape from the stresses of Meadowsview.

Always there for me, she'd been the voice of reason. She was logical and straightforward, yet soft-spoken and kind. But here, in her private sanctuary, she now knew my greatest secret. Would she judge me? See me in a different way? My mind was awash with too many questions. *Jesus. What does she think of me at this moment?*

"Warms up fast," she said, breaking the silence.

"Yeah, that didn't take long," I agreed.

She unrolled a sleeping bag, then reached under the table for two square pillows. "C'mere," she said. "Get comfortable. I have some time, and we need to talk."

I sat beside her. "I wanted to tell you—I did. You were the one person I knew I should talk to, but I couldn't."

"Why? That's what I don't understand. You'd be the first one I would come to."

"Well, technically, you *are* the first one I came to."

"I've been worried. And even now, you seem different." She eased her head down on one pillow, then tapped the other with her hand. "Like I said, get comfortable." Reaching for my shirt-collar, she pulled me down beside her.

"I don't want your sympathy, Kate. I mean, if that's what this is all about. It's probably the last thing I need right now."

"I don't do sympathy," she replied.

"Good. Cause I don't..."

"You just don't know when to be quiet, do you?"

In all the time we'd known each other, we'd never kissed. There were those friendly pecks on the cheek at social occasions, or when we hadn't seen each other in a long time, but she'd always been beyond reach. She was off limits, and I would only have complicated her life. My bad habits, lack of regimen, and disregard for convention would have eventually come between us. But she was a sight to behold. I knew the subtle curves of her features, her smile, her eyes, and each delicate line beside them.

When our lips met, the raw chemistry between us was undeniable. Tender. Passionate. Told.

As she pulled away, and rose to her knees, I could hear my heart beat. And with a stare that dared me to look away, she began unbuttoning her blouse. Unable to hide the bashful blush in her cheeks, she removed her top, then stood.

Wearing only a bra and panties, she stared at me, knowing that this day would never be forgotten. There was no going back. Brazenly, she reached behind her and unlatched her bra, which slid from her shoulders to the floor.

Captivating. Hypnotizing. The auburn in her hair shimmered in the lamplight, which threw seductive shadows on the walls behind her. She was more alluring than any woman I'd ever known, and I couldn't take my eyes off of her.

With a taunting smile, she tucked her thumbs under the waistband of her panties, and raised an eyebrow. She then turned her gaze from my eyes to my pants, which I eagerly removed.

Taking her hands in mine, I pulled her down, close to me, where she nestled her face in the curve of my neck and put her hand on my chest.

"You know this is a game changer, right?" She moved her hand from my chest to my chin, making me look at her. "I'm not one of your Hollywood girls..."

"No. You're not." In all honesty, at that moment I would've said anything to touch her. But it was the truth. She was breathtaking, and what followed was beyond words. Nothing could compare to the rushes she sent through me with the touch of her warm skin.

— — —

"Dorothy," the voice whispered. "Dorothy."

Leah awakened to the smiling face she knew as Scarecrow. The room was spacious, and the bed she lay upon was covered with a silk canopy which draped to the floor.

"Welcome." It was the voice of the girl who had called to her. "Welcome to Nevaeh." From the far side of the room, she stepped from the shadows cast by a single torch. About Leah's age, she was of royal blood, wearing a purple satin gown that accented her red hair and hazel eyes. Her skin was pale, cheeks were flush, and she spoke with a Gaelic accent—much different than that of hills.

Sitting up in the large bed, Leah looked around the massive quarters, then finally back to the smiling eyes of the other girl. "Who are you?" she asked.

"Emily," the girl answered, and approached the bedside.

"I'll be close by," Kris said, then disappeared into a dimly lit corridor.

"You're the one who told me to beware." Leah looked down, ashamed for ignoring the warning.

"Yes. I did."

───────

We approached the main path, where we tried to collect ourselves. And after straightening our clothes and hair, we continued back to the hospital.

"You have no idea what it was like for me meeting your flavor of the month. I mean, I wanted to strangle you sometimes. But I just looked at them and smiled, thinking 'this one will last about a week, or this one may make it til the end of the semester.' And I was always dead-on."

"I never knew that. You always just seemed so..."

"Choose your words carefully," she smiled.

"Umm... unattainable?"

"Unattainable? So that's what you're going with? Seriously? Did you ever consider that maybe I just didn't wanna be another notch in your belt."

"I don't put notches in my belt—I get a new one."

"Exactly," she responded. "But why didn't you even try? Would it have hurt you to at least feign interest?"

"I was interested, and you knew it. But it was like we decided early on to keep things friendly. You had plans, and they didn't include me. Let's face it, I would've held you back."

"Held me back? Did it ever occur to you that maybe I was hoping you'd rescue me?"

"From what? You had it made."

"Had it made? Really? And my reward for having it made is a room at Meadowsview? I *live* in a hospital. You think I have it made? Do you know how many times I wished I was more like you?"

"Like me?"

"A wild card."

"I don't know what's funnier, you thinking I'm a wild card, or wanting to be more like me because of it."

"Okay. So maybe that's not the right word. A free spirit. You weren't afraid of missing a test, or getting your heart broken. I was the exact opposite. Sheltered, expected to be a doctor... for as long as I remember, my life was all mapped out for me."

"I always thought you *wanted* to be a doctor."

"I did, but I wanted the choice to be mine—to at least be free to make a bad decision."

"Is that what *this* was? A bad decision?"

"No," she answered. "This was me, being with you." She walked slower. "This was me going against the grain of everything that's been drilled into me my entire life. That's what I meant when I said you were a wild card. You could change my way of thinking. Change *me*."

"Why would I change you? You're the one who has a grip on things. Let's face it, I'm the one who's always been a train wreck. You were definitely better off without me, and untouchable, way out of my league."

"Out of your league? What is it with men and leagues? Divisions? Here's a newsflash—there are no leagues, just people. And the divisions are only in your mind."

"I only meant that..."

"I know what you meant," she said. "But now that you've touched me, I'm not so untouchable, am I? The thing is..." She drew a deep breath, then slowly exhaled. "What you never realized... or maybe I just concealed it well... is that you touched me a long time ago."

I wanted to tell her, and she deserved to hear me say it, but I couldn't. Only a few nights before then, I was seriously contemplating suicide, and those three words would change everything. How could I pull her into the chaos around me?

"It's okay," she said, then stopped walking. "But just for the record, I've always known."

"Known what?"

"That you love me." She turned away, then straight back. "And I'm pretty sure you've always known I love you too."

"Yes," I answered. "So does that make us liars, or just in denial?"

"Maybe both. Maybe neither." She twisted her hair. "Maybe it just means the timing wasn't right."

"We've always been so different," I said. "Polar opposites."

"True. But in some ways—the important things—we usually see eye-to-eye. But how do you see me now? I mean, what I really wanna know is, now that..."

I stepped in front of her and put my hands around her waist. "Choose your words carefully," I grinned and pulled her closer. "You're beautiful. Beyond compare."

Chapter 12 - The Elijah Wave

Doing our best to appear professional—as though we hadn't spent a good part of the morning in each other's arms—we were greeted by a somewhat austere Dr. Young.

"Well," he looked at us as though he knew exactly what we'd been up to, then grinned when he noticed Kathleen's blouse was buttoned wrong. "You may want to fix that, Dr. Scott."

Despite our attempts to appear innocent, it was obvious that we'd done more than merely taken a walk. But he exercised the good taste of not putting too fine a point on it. "While you two were out, Jon ran an MRI on Elijah."

"What?" Back in her element, she immediately protested, "Why wasn't I informed?"

"Well, Dr. Scott, perhaps if you'd been taking calls

you would have known."

She discreetly gripped the phone in her pocket, and with noticeably blush cheeks, faced me.

"You sure seem to be in good spirits, David," he said. "Maybe you two should get out more often." Having tactfully admonished us, he turned to her. "Jon needs to see you in the Imaging Lab. At your convenience, of course," he sarcastically finished, then continued his stroll through the hallway.

"God, I can't believe I did that." She fixed her blouse.

"I wouldn't worry about it too much."

"No, you don't understand, Ian's one of my father's oldest friends—they talk all the time. I wouldn't be surprised if they're already discussing it."

As I followed her to the third floor, she continued. "Ya know, it took me three months to realize that one of the reasons my father was so adamant about me coming here was so his 'old pal' could keep an eye on me." Laughing, she resentfully finished. "Nice, huh? I mean, I know it's with good intentions, but sometimes I feel like a sixteen-year-old."

"Yeah, he always seemed to call the shots. But I guess that's the price you pay, huh?"

"Pay for what? Oh, for being a doctor's daughter. Is that what you mean?" she smirked. "It's the price I pay for my lavish lifestyle?"

"Well, that *was* a pretty sweet condo in Hollywood, ya gotta admit that."

"It did have a great view," she said as we entered the Imaging Lab, where Jon was looking at scans of Elijah's MRI.

"Odd," he greeted us as he closely examined the transparencies.

"What's odd? What is it? Aren't these Leah's scans?" She seemed sure they were.

"Actually, no, they're Elijah's."

"But, this mark, are you sure Jon?"

"Come on, Kathleen. I'm a neurosurgeon, not an intern," he answered with his usual derision, then pulled Leah's scans from a steel cabinet and hung one beside Elijah's. They were almost identical.

"Jon, this can't be right—look at the spot here." She pointed to the small nodule, about the size of a pencil tip, located in the exact position as the one in Leah's.

"There are a few differences, like here, in the parietal lobe, and here, the frontal." He pointed to areas in both scans.

"Still," Kathleen said, "the similarities are amazing."

"Not unusual in identical twins," he said, "but with fraternal twins, exceedingly rare. And I'd sure like to know what that is." Perplexed. Intrigued. He tapped his index finger on the spot in question.

"Dr Scott, Dr. Weston and Dr. Svelgaard, please come to the Conference Room." The address came from a room speaker.

"Well, Dr. Weston, shall we? Jon, you coming?"

"Of course. When he calls, we jump... but you two go ahead. I won't be long."

We entered the Conference Room and were greeted by Rebecca, Annie and Dr. Young.

"Okay, we're all here. Wait, we still need Jon." Biding

time, he looked at his notes.

Through the window I noticed that the sky had become much darker, as thunderheads rolled ominously above the landscape.

Moments later, Dr. Svelgaard came in and appeared, as usual, to be inconvenienced by his summon to the conference room.

The King began. "I apologize for giving no prior notice of this meeting, but we're here regarding this evening's procedure. Also, our anesthesiologist was called away, but he'll be back in time to sedate Elijah at seven. That should provide ample time to get them prepped and begin by eight." With everyone's complete attention, he continued. "The five of you will be conducting a test to be headed by Dr. Weston." He pointed in my direction. "David will delegate to each of you, and then assess the results, which will be reported to me tomorrow morning. Now, Dr. Weston, tell us what you need."

"My laptop," I answered directly. "All of the monitoring equipment already in use will be fed into it. We'll continue to watch all vital signs." I looked into the faces of the others, who nodded in agreement, and then to Jon. "Additionally, we'll be targeting specific brain activity. Dr. Svelgaard, could you help with the calibrations and sensor attachment?" I made a peace offering.

"Of course," he responded.

"Dr. Scott, you'll be watching for similarities between them—heartbeat, blood pressure..." I tried not to smile, looking squarely at the woman who was just as beautiful in her blue frock as she was bare breasted upon me earlier.

"What about me?" Rebecca asked, wanting to know exactly how she would contribute.

Annie, who had quietly observed, teasingly followed. "Yeah, David, and what do *I* get to do?"

"I'm getting to you guys," I grinned. Outwardly, I appeared confident, of sound bearing, but my hands shook in my lap, and I was well aware that we were blindly sailing into uncharted waters, I at the helm.

Despite certain differences in opinions or beliefs, we were noted professionals preparing to conduct a test that was clearly not your typical, run-of-the-mill, medical procedure. Of course, no one used the word 'telepathy', but it was understood that we were exploring what I hoped would be a deep subconscious connection between the twins.

I faced Kathleen. She was the only one who knew that my composure was an act, and that I was actually tense and apprehensive. "Our specific task is noting, not only similarities, but also differences. We'll have several waves to watch all at once."

Except for Dr. Svelgaard, there was a noticeable sense of camaraderie at the round table. And though we didn't know it then, each of us, including Jon, would be deeply affected by what we would witness later that night.

"Annie, you and I will monitor REM patterns and Delta waves, and Rebecca, you'll operate our audio-video equipment."

"Cool," she answered, "I used to work in a portrait studio." The vitality she brought to the table was worth her weight in gold.

"Very good then," Dr Young nodded. "And are there any questions?"

"Yes," Jon replied. "What are we hoping to achieve? I mean, if you ask me... "

Dr. Young interrupted him, "We're *not* asking you Jon. And like it or not, you *will* be a part of this." His blunt statement and curt smile left the Swede biting his tongue.

"Well, maybe I can answer that, if you don't mind." I looked to the King for approval.

"Go right ahead." He leaned back in the black leather chair, and placed both hands behind his head.

"First, we're hoping to determine if they share similar dream patterns. We'll be comparing an array of brain activity... Second, by monitoring her twin," I glanced at the neurosurgeon, "we can assess how significant the similarities, or differences, between their waves are."

"Yes, but can't this be done by simply monitoring the boy with an EKG?" Jon was a stubborn one.

"Actually, no. By having both of them in the same environment, with the same external stimulus, I think we'll get a truer comparison."

"And why in the world would you monitor differences?" He was relentless.

"Polarity," I answered, referring to a section of my theory. But, having tacit understanding of Jon's cynical nature, I appeased him as much as possible, skipping around terms associated with my research. After all, he was a respected leader and gifted surgeon, and despite his bad attitude and lack of social skills, I really wanted him to be a part of this.

It was clear to me that we were dealing with some of those unknown forces which had become a pillar of my studies. And the Goforth Situation provided a rare opportunity to conduct a test that could yield a great harvest of data.

After a few more minutes, Dr. Young closed the meeting. "Okay then. I'll expect the results on my desk in the morning."

―――

"Are you from England?" Leah asked, curious about Emily's accent.

"No. Wales," she answered. "In the mountains."

"I live in the mountains too. Or used to."

"I know, in the Appalachians of West Virginia. Mine are called the Snowdonias."

Inept at friendship, Leah looked shyly around the room, and after a quiet moment when neither of them knew what to say, "But why are you here?" she asked.

"Because I have to be," Emily said. "But more importantly," she tilted her head slightly to one side, "do you know why *you're* here?" Her voice went from that of a young girl to one of insight. "Do you know why you've come to Nevaeh?"

"I'm dreaming, ain't I?"

"Well, yes. But do you know why you're here?"

"No, I went the wrong way before, so we came back this way," Leah responded.

"Think back," Emily said, "back to the day you were in church. When you and Elijah were talk-talking."

How does she know about our talk-talk? Leah was at

first surprised, but then stared blankly through the canopy, recalling that fateful day...

It was many months before, during the winter, and the church was cold, but, as always, filled to capacity with Jacob's followers. Bundled in well-worn coats, the twins stood in the front row—the only appropriate place for the family of the 'Good Reverend'.

Naomi, who rarely missed a sermon, was absent this particular evening, as she was tending to other needs.

Lets talk-talk. Leah turned slightly toward her brother, who, with a hand in front of his face, smiled when she suggested, *Lets talk-talk backwards! I'll tell you what to say!*

The twins knew King James backwards and sideways, upwards and downwards. Exceptional readers, something enforced by Jacob, they sometimes reversed the letters of each word as they read to each other.

Leah, she thought. *Say it backwards.*

"Hael!" Elijah blurted, and raised his hands like the others did when they spoke in Tongues.

Surprised, several of the flock then joined in his praise, clapping and shouting "Halleluiah" and "Glory be!"

Praise God! she blasted the thought enthusiastically.

"Esiarp Dog!" he shouted, imitating her excitement.

While his following joined in praise, Jacob merely watched suspiciously. And when she noticed his disapproving gaze, she sent one final thought...

"I ssim eht dlo yddad," Leah said, lowering her arms.

I do too, he thought, briefly facing his twin.

When the service ended, a silent Jacob, followed closely by his children, walked to his car and drove down the winding road home.

"What was that?" He looked in the rearview mirror at Leah, who was usually the one he blamed.

"What was what?" she answered innocently.

As they entered their house, Jacob removed his belt and asked again, "What was that display? How dare you mock the Lord!"

Leah shuddered at the memory, and Emily placed an assuring hand on her shoulder. "It's alright. You're safe in Nevaeh. But do you remember what you and Elijah were doing in church that night?"

"We were talking backwards."

"Yes... and Nevaeh..."

"Is Heaven," Leah stated. "It's heaven backwards." Aware of the implications of her journey, "So, I'm dead? And this is Heaven?" she asked.

"No," Emily smiled. "But it's not far away."

Who would look after Elijah? "What does 'not far away' mean?"

"It means you're very close..." Emily answered. "For most, there's a single crossing, but for you there's more." She tilted her head curiously. "And I've been wondering why you've come to the Southern Gate."

Her eyes then turned from hazel to black, and like small monitors, reflected Leah's memory, but from perspectives she hadn't seen.

The first was that of the attending nurse at Huntington Hills on the night she fell into her coma.

"Whatever it was... it must've been horrifying," Emily

said. "Whatever it was that caused you to give up..."

She paused, giving Leah a chance to respond, and when she didn't, she blinked her eyes, flashing forward. "And this is when you were on the train bridge." Her left eye showed Elijah in the distance, and her right eye showed Leah hanging from the slats. "Why didn't he help?" she asked.

"Because I made him promise... I made him promise not to talk-talk anymore." Leah raised her fingertips to her lips. "And he didn't want to break a promise..." She closed her eyes and turned away. "No more. I'm done with the past. Can we just move on?"

"Of course... I'm sorry... Of course we can move on, if you're sure that's what you want..."

Leah merely nodded.

"Further in Nevaeh, there are three more bridges."

"More?"

"Yes, three more." Her eyes revealed the next crossing, a burning bridge which spanned a river surrounded by darkness.

"But if this is Heaven, why are there more bridges?"

In a blink, her eyes were again hazel. "Because you have to go through the levels."

"The levels? What levels?"

Emily rotated her wrist in circles, producing a piece of yellowed parchment, which she unrolled on the bed.

Placing an index finger on the top of the page to keep it from curling, Leah viewed the ancient map, labeled in large script, 'The Levels of Ascension'.

"Here," Emily said, pointing to the lower edge of the map, "this is where we are." Near her finger was a small fortress, and beside it was written, 'The Southern Entry.'

I arrived early, surprised to find that Jon had already begun attaching the sensors and was waiting for me.

"You'll probably want to check those." He nodded once in the direction of each twin.

"I'm sure they're fine, I'll just..." I repositioned one. "Tweak them a little."

"Tweak away, this is your big top tonight." He persisted in making sure I knew he believed we were wasting our time.

Kathleen and Annie showed up punctually at eight and were greeted by Rebecca, who was clearly excited. "This is going to be so cool!" She was thrilled to be helping out in any way.

"Yeah, whatever." Jon reviewed the initial readings, glancing frequently at the monitors, as he tried to appear as aloof as possible.

I positioned a tripod in a corner and placed a digital recorder on it. "Rebecca, this is Record." I tapped the top of the device. "And this is Zoom." I touched the back. "Get full views of both children." I stepped around her. "And that's a backup power supply." I pointed to the corner, then faced the others. "Wait, I almost forgot." I turned back to Rebecca. "Only press Record once. Just let it run."

Raising an index finger, she confirmed, "Uno."

With the twins and team prepped and ready to go, I asserted my direction. "Okay. We covered this earlier. We're looking for relative signals. Relative can be either similar or opposite." I avoided eye contact with Jon, and continued, "Their usual signals will show up the same as always, but the target sensors will feed directly into my laptop, and the program will look for direct or polar correlations."

Stepping in front of the camera, I nodded as an anxious Rebecca pressed Record and I looked into the lens. "Subjects are Leah and Elijah Goforth." I turned to the curious looks of the others, then we took our positions.

The storm began with a single crash of thunder, followed immediately by strong gusts of rain against the building.

Kathleen and I exchanged a discreet glance. And with a million questions in our eyes, we both turned to the windows, to the downpour that had been building throughout the day.

For the first forty-five minutes the data reflected few parallels between the children. Their pulses were different, brain waves different, and there were no real similarities, not even notable opposites. But then Elijah began to dream.

I sat beside Annie with my hands behind my head, watching the twins, as she sat with her eyes glued to the laptop monitor. "David." She leaned closer to the screen, where a small icon flashed between the twins' compared heart-rates. At intervals of about five seconds, a single unusual beat rhythmically pulsed higher than the others on both readouts. It could have been coincidence, but it wasn't. The icon continued to flash, and within moments another icon appeared. 'Optic nerve signals'. Then another and another, as one-by-one Elijah's signals began to match those of his sister. *Jesus. They're identical.*

"Rebecca, zoom in on this monitor," I said.

"God!" she responded, looking through the recorder's viewfinder.

Leah tried to hide her emotions. She stared at the parchment while Emily showed her the route she would take, noticing the change in her guest's expression.

"Are you okay?" she asked, looking to Leah with uncertainty.

"Yes, I'm fine," she lied. She felt her brother's presence, but didn't want to believe that he would ever break his word.

"Beyond the fiery bridge is..." Emily stopped, and quickly stood.

"Elijah! What are you doing? You shouldn't *be* here!"

"We're not evil!" he said. "I'm taking you back!" The look on his face was unwavering, as he began to talk-talk. *Come back with me Leah. I miss you.*

"No Elijah, I can't, and we can't talk-talk anymore. I already *told* you!"

Unsure of how to deal with the unexpected arrival at the Southern Entry, Emily picked up the parchment, and it disappeared in her hand.

Eerily alike, it was clear that what Kris and Karen had

said about their eye movements was undeniable, and with their heads now shaved they looked like mirrored images.

We all watched the twins laying side by side, their monitors reflecting identical pulses, blood pressure, and Delta waves. It was as if the equipment was tracking one person.

When Jon checked the leads, and shook his head in disbelief, I grinned, having often seen cynics respond to the paranormal. And he was undoubtedly a cynic.

"Still don't believe in telepathy, Jon?" There. I *said* it. Someone had to sooner or later.

He finally relented. "I have no explanation." Of course he didn't, no one did. It was something beyond explanation, regardless of terminology, expertise or his own smug beliefs.

As I looked into their silent and stunned faces, I understood the significance of 'The Elijah Wave'. It was clear that the connection between the twins was much deeper than any of us had imagined—they not only looked alike, but their minds were wired almost identically. What we were witnessing was indisputable evidence of a psychic connection between them.

It had been difficult to consider my budding theory until then, but with proof that they were connected, I made the statement. "It's possible that the spots in their MRI's could serve as some sort of relay between them." Hearing myself say it, the idea seemed more plausible, yet I felt like I was grasping at straws.

Expecting a barrage of smiles and laughter, I was surprised to look up and see that each of them was looking directly in my eyes—even Jon.

Speechless, he held only brief eye contact before turning away without comment.

I recalled his much different attitude during the morning procedure. But I didn't say anything. Why rub it in? His stricken expression was the only vindication that I needed. After all, the findings of recent days had only proven that modern science couldn't explain the Goforth Situation. *His* method had failed, and though he tried to come across as unaffected—checking sensors and performing standard procedures—he was stripped of his usual arrogance, refuted.

Each of us reacted in our own way.

Annie quietly watched, as though analyzing the twins as they slept. Her stare went from Elijah to Leah, then to the laptop, where the flashing lights on one side of the monitor were in perfect synch with those on the other.

Kathleen watched the twins and their signals. Alert, discerning, she stood at the foot of Leah's bed, turning frequently to glance at the screen in front of me.

Rebecca beamed like a Hollywood director. Not knowing I was watching, she whispered to herself, "No fucking way..."

While Meadowsview was being pounded by an intense storm—an anomaly of its own—we witnessed an event that would one day be lauded in professional journals. Here was the proof that would silence all but the most closed-minded critics of telepathy. In short, many important theories—including WTF—were now validated, proven.

A rush of adrenaline shot through my veins, but I kept

my composure. "Rebecca, are you getting this?"

"Yes, Doctor," she answered.

Shaken by sudden cannon-like jolts of thunder, the third floor lights flickered.

"Their monitors!" Seeing that the screens had gone black, Kathleen stepped toward Leah. She then froze when another, even louder series of booms caused the lights to go completely out.

We all gasped.

In the dark, with a raging battle exploding in the sky above, we were unprepared for what followed...

The emergency light over the door suddenly came on, and the twins were sitting up in their beds.

One side of their faces was lit by the backup light, and the other was lit only by more frequent flashes of lightning through the window. Entranced, they stared ahead.

Petrified, with gaping eyes, we watched and waited.

And with a break in the thunder, "Emoc kcab Hael," Elijah said, sounding strangely normal. He then fell back into his bed, and Leah did the same.

When the power was restored, nobody said a word. Exchanging only incidental glances, we tried to make sense of what we'd just seen.

And one-by-one, just as they had come, the flashing icons on my laptop disappeared.

Chapter 13 – Nevaeh

"Jesus!" Rebecca, with her usual fervor, broke the silence in what was a very tense room. "God, I've never seen anything like that in my entire life. I can't wait to see the video."

Along with undeniable proof of dream-sharing, there were new, unexpected, questions to add to the equation.

Jon made several attempts to revive Leah, certain that this was the perfect time. "If she can sit up, she can *wake* up." Using every conceivable method, he failed to gain even a minimal response. All indications were that she was in the same state as before. "We should do another Glasgow," he uttered in frustration.

"It'll be interesting to see what Elijah draws," Kathleen said.

Trying to piece together all I'd been told, read, and now witnessed, her words hit a chord. It was a damned good question. *What will Elijah draw... and what am I missing?*

"How long will he be out?" I asked.

"At least another hour or so. Why?"

Wanting a few minutes to look at his drawings, I went straight to the door.

"David?" Kathleen followed me. "What about your computer and the recorder?"

"Right." I turned to Jon. "Would you mind..."

"Not at all," he answered, and began removing the twins' sensors.

"So, do I just turn it off now?" Rebecca asked.

"Yeah, I think we have what we need," I answered.

The results were certain to be interesting, and I was anxious to run the program, but Elijah's drawings were now brought to the forefront of the Goforth Situation.

— — —

"But Leah, I miss you. Come back so we can watch the train and…"

"And *what*, Elijah? Be afraid forever? No thanks!"

Knowing that she had only two choices, she was determined to continue the journey, and knew that time was limited.

Sections of Elijah's body expanded and contracted, trying to unite, but repelling each other like magnets of the same polarity. Resembling a shaky hologram, he was outlined by random blue sparks that arched and fell quickly to the stone floor.

He'd managed to get a foothold in his sister's dream, but it was lost when she abruptly scolded him.

"Go back Elijah! Go! I don't *want* you here!"

She'd never, not once in her life, turned him away, and it sent a chill through him that was beyond compare. Even his father's cruelty paled in the sudden shadow cast by his sister's words.

Rejected, the sparks around him grew faint, and his image more and more transparent, until he completely disappeared.

Though his wounded expression hurt, with tearful resolve, Leah commanded, "Show me the last three. Tell me what I have to do." Her swollen eyes reflecting a lifetime of submission, in a whisper, she finished, "I have to keep going."

Swirling her hand, Emily once again presented the parchment.

Unaware that we were in the hallway, and still within an ear's shot, "Everything appears to be functioning properly," Jon said. Desperately clinging to his disbelief in the paranormal, despite having witnessed it in person, his tone was defenseless, out of character for a man who had made a life of studying the human mind. "Maybe there's really something to it," he added. "But how?"

Annie listened without reply, knowing Jon would decide for himself whether or not he'd seen something extraordinary.

"So now what? You're gonna rifle through his pictures again?" Kathleen asked.

"It makes sense," I answered. "*You* saw that. We all

saw it. There's a connection, but we're missing something. It's gotta be there in his drawings." There was renewed conviction in my voice, the kind that only comes with a measure of encouragement.

She watched as I frantically spread the pages across his table. *Bridges, bridges... I've seen these... Wait...* Stepping around her, I hovered like an engineer over a blueprint, awed by the detail he'd placed in the unfinished picture. His second portrayal of Goforth's Crossing was from a different perspective and large areas had been left untouched, as though he was waiting to fill them in later.

I stared at the piece for several minutes, looking for clues. *Covered bridge, sunset, bare trees.* Committing the words to memory, I faced her.

"They're bringing him back. Hurry," she urged.

Quickly stacking the drawings, I returned them to their place, then something else caught my notice...

The small wooden box under Elijah's pillow barely reflected the fluorescent light. To *not* look wasn't a second thought—not after the night we'd had—and so I picked it up and looked at the lid, which was carved with the detail of a barn owl. Staring into its lifelike eyes, I then looked inside.

In the hallway, we stood clear as Rebecca returned Elijah to his room. "Your camera and laptop are in the corner," she said as she passed.

With Kathleen following, I returned to her room, where I looked at Leah and then through the windows. Waning thunder resounded infrequently in the east, and the gales were now reduced to droplets which quietly streaked the windowpanes. Through patches in the night sky, random streaks of moonlight lit the countryside.

"I need coffee," I said, and picked up my equipment.

"Tell ya what," she responded, "take your things upstairs and I'll bring some in a minute."

"You know this might take awhile?" Knowing the procedure required several steps, "Ready for a long night?" I asked.

"We'll see," Kathleen whispered, and opened the stairway door.

— — —

"Nevaeh is vast, as big as the universe," Emily began. "This map is of only a very small part, the entry and levels."

"But you said there were *two* entries," Leah said.

"Yes, the north entry leads directly to Lanrete Efil, but where we are leads through the Levels of Ascension." She dragged a fingertip across the parchment. "The levels are joined by three spans... Erif Crossing, The Span of Epoh Sevil, and..." she placed a finger on the northernmost crossing, "The Rise of Lanrete Efil."

"For those who are ready to enter the Kingdom, only the last bridge matters, but some are unsure and need more time."

"Do *I* need more time?" Leah looked innocently at Emily and then at the map.

"You have one foot in Nevaeh, and still one in life. But by the time you reach the northern pass, you'll know."

Leah tried to appear unaffected by her brother's appearance, while Emily considered its impact.

"There are three rules you must follow," she finally stated. "You must go alone, stay on the purple stone path…"

"Like the yellow brick road," Kris interrupted with his comforting manner.

"From the Heather Hills, you'll see the fire of Erif Crossing," Emily said. "And remember, nothing in Nevaeh can harm you." She then let the map curl, and with a snap of her fingers it disappeared. "And the last rule… you can only tell truths, a lie will take steps away. Sleep now. You have to leave at daybreak."

Kathleen arrived with two large cups of coffee, which she placed on a nightstand before falling across the bed. "I could sleep for days," she said, reaching beside the bed. "Missing something?" She rolled to her back. "Nice phone. You have a few messages, ya know?"

"How many?" I grinned, having, as usual, been avoiding calls.

"Only, wow, eighteen messages. Good to know I'm not the *only* one you ignore," she added.

"Any text messages?" I asked, knowing that my phone would block all but those from a select few.

"Three," she answered and placed the phone on the nightstand.

As I booted my laptop she turned to lay lengthwise. Propping her head, she watched me for a moment before asking, "So, you planning to check your messages, or what?"

"I hadn't really thought about it." Baiting her, I smiled to myself, knowing her standard for efficiency.

"Aren't you afraid you'll miss something important?" She shook her head. "I mean, really, why even have it if you don't use it?"

"I do use it, I've got like four-hundred eighty-three songs and a few movies. I use it all the time."

"It's a phone, not an entertainment center. I can't believe you. I'd be worried about missing a call, but not you—you just put everything on autopilot and hope it's all smooth sailing."

"Okay, give it to me." With a brief gaze, I held out my hand. "Let me show you something. Voice mail?" I said as she placed it in my palm, "I don't really use it."

"Oh, that's quite apparent," she smirked.

"Everyone knows to text me, so I just kind of review and delete voice mail. Like this." I mimicked the callers. "David, your dry cleaning's ready... *Delete*. Hey David, we're meeting at the club... *Delete*..."

"Well, *I* never knew to text you," she interrupted. "But I guess I'm not 'everyone', am I?"

Ignoring the remark, I opened the messages.

The first was from John. *Dali destroyed neighbor's birdbath. You're paying the bill.* The other two were reminders from Kelli, and left my face flush. *Saturday night, seven o'clock. Wear tux. Be sober.* She wasn't one to waste words, as her second text said only *SAOT*, which I knew meant 'Sober and on time'.

"What is it?" Kathleen asked.

"I have to get back to LA."

Knowing he was there late, at 1:20 Friday morning, Annie hesitated before finally tapping on Dr. Young's door.

When he opened it, she began with a sense of urgency. "I think we should give David the Llewellyn file."

"You what?" Dr Young laughed as he closed the door behind them. "Absolutely not. We have legal responsibilities." He laughed again. "Annie, you of all people should understand the delicate balance here. Dr. Weston is not subject to our internal, and very private, client information." It was final.

Her face written with dissatisfaction, Annie wasn't one to give up without a fight. "I suppose I could take some of those built-up vacation days." Smirking, she was well aware that he needed her.

"What? You wouldn't. You're bluffing. Hell, I've been trying to give you time off for four years."

In a decisive tone, "Don't put money on it," Annie said, and then turned to face the door. "I bet Acapulco would be nice this winter," she added, challenging her superior.

"Well 'Bon voyage', or maybe 'Adios' is more appropriate."

Going through the motions of leaving, she went to the door. "If there's something more that we can give Dr. Weston, anything else we can add to his ability to assess this case, I think we're compelled to provide it."

"But unless I'm mistaken, Dr. Weston doesn't underwrite Meadowsview's insurance, does he?"

"Oh, come on—I'm not suggesting you give him level six clearance, for God's sake."

"That's *exactly* what you're suggesting!"

"But with the test results and what happened tonight..."

"Results I've not seen yet," he chimed, then turned to the the window. "Looks like the rain's gone," he said, keeping his back turned while he considered the decision.

"Yes. But another storm's coming," Annie replied.

Staring into the night, he took a different tone. "You know I've always tried to be supportive of your choices. Remember the kitten?"

She too looked solemnly through the window. "She loved that cat."

"What was its name? Something really strange..."

"Franklin," she managed a faint smile. "She said it looked like Benjamin Franklin."

"Yes, yes," he smiled as he looked over his shoulder. "Whatever happened to Franklin?"

"One of the nurses took him home," she said, recalling the times Emily sat in her office with the kitten on her lap.

"I hate to think you'd withhold something that could help with this case, Ian."

"Surely you're not questioning my integrity?" His disappointed tone was followed with a reprimanding stare. "You're assuming an awful lot here." Slightly raising his voice, he continued, "The state of the twins has nothing to do with Emily Llewellyn. And," he finished sternly, "you're well aware that her file was sealed at the family's request."

"You weren't there tonight, Ian. I *was*. They sat up. *Both* of them—just like *she* did. And yes, I'm all too aware of Meadowsview's legal responsibilities. But for just once try to think on another level." Appealing to her longtime friend, she finished, "What's in her file could help David to help us, and I know you'll do the right thing once you realize how stubborn you're being."

"Stubborn? You're talking about breaking a confidence that could severely cripple this institute. So forgive me if I don't share your enthusiasm. And can I trust that you've not discussed this with David?"

"Of course not. But I think it's the right thing to do."

"I'll give him the file when he gives me his report. Fair enough?"

"Yes, fair enough," she answered and gripped the doorknob. "And I'll make sure he gives you a report. Just have that file ready."

———

Wearing a white tunic bound by a rope sash, Leah hesitantly took a step. "I wish you could come too." Her pleading eyes were faintly lit in the first light of the Nevaeh dawn.

Kris placed a hand on her small shoulder. "You'll be fine," he said. "Nothing here can hurt you."

"Remember to cross the last bridge before the sun sets at Lanrete Efil," Emily said with a concerned tone. "And stay on the path."

Contemplative and unsure, Leah began across the purple stones leading her deeper into Nevaeh. A light mist caused the surrounding foliage to glisten, presenting a tranquil landscape which helped move her along the path.

Before entering a dense grove of trees, she paused and turned back to the compassionate smiles of her friends.

"Go, child," Kris encouraged. "Go now and cross your bridges."

"When?" Kathleen asked. "How soon do you have to go?"

"The dinner's tomorrow, but I need to be at the airport this morning."

"This couldn't come at a worse time," she scowled. "I mean, you're bolting when we need you the most."

Knowing she was right—the test results now being more important than ever—I tried to assure her. "Look, I'll finish running the program, print a preliminary report for Dr. Young, then do the detailed comps on the plane. I'll call you with the results."

"Yeah, okay David." She wasn't convinced. "Whatever. As long as you have something to give him this morning." Outwardly Kathleen gave the impression that the twins were her only concern, but there was an undertone in her voice that rang on a more personal note, causing me to weigh my options.

"What if I come back next week?"

"Would you?"

"Why, anything for you, darlin."

Exactly what she wanted to hear, she pulled me close. "Well, yes, that *is* the correct answer. And ye shall be generously rewarded."

--- --- ---

Every imaginable shade of green existed within the folds of Leah's Nevaeh. It draped the trees and tinted the grass, and lush patches surrounded the purple stones, defining the trail vividly.

The path before her widened, revealing a valley through which a faraway river flowed for many miles. *"From the Heather Hills, you'll see the fire of Erif Crossing."* She remembered Emily's words clearly.

To the right, the valley was light and warm, but to the left, dark and threatening. Flames engulfed the distant bridge, casting red and yellow reflections in the water beneath it.

Just my luck, she thought, *the bridge is on the dark side.* She drew several deep breaths before bearing directly toward the fiery crossing.

"Don't be afraid of the dark," her mother had said. "Because I'll always light your way."

Leah knew Naomi had tried desperately to appeal to Jacob, but there were too many memories of times when her mother just gave in and allowed his displaced anger.

Moving quickly across the stones, she stepped into the valley, slowing as she remembered her mother's words.

"But where are you *now*?" she said aloud. "You said you'd light the way, but where are you now?" In an angry whisper, she finished, "I hate you for dying."

Leah immediately found herself back on the hillside where she was before, staring from the same place, into the same valley.

"You can only tell truths, a lie will take steps away," Emily had warned.

"Okay. Okay, I didn't mean that. I don't hate you." She hoped the truth would return her to where she was, but it didn't. *Guess it doesn't work that way. Only the truth from now on,* she thought, and began again toward the dark side of Nevaeh.

We were on the verge of falling asleep when I opened my eyes to flashing lights on my computer screen. The initial diagnostics were close to being complete, so I gently lifted her arm as Kathleen, clearly exhausted, clutched a pillow and rolled to her other side.

John's program, which he designed per my specifications, had taken many months to create, and I was confident in its abilities. I watched the screen for several minutes, sipping the lukewarm coffee, and recalling the painstaking hours of entering data.

Finally the endless rows of moving symbols stopped and the title, 'Prime Ass'—my brother's clever abbreviation for 'Primary Associations'—appeared at the top of the page.

I opened a blank document, then copied and pasted the words on the screen. Thirty-one nouns and verbs, these were the words from which phrases would be made.

Covered bridge, sunset, bare trees... I remembered Elijah's drawing, and typed the words in.

"How's it going?" Kathleen turned again and was facing me with her eyes closed.

"It's going," I answered, adding the phrase 'Emoc kcab hael' to the page.

— — —

Leah recalled a private moment with her mother...

"I know it's hard having Elijah as your brother," Naomi's voice was always gentle and loving. "But I've watched you, and you're the best sister he could ever have."

The sincerity in the way she said it made Leah smile.

"He's really smart, mommy. And I hate the way they call him names and laugh at him, especially at church."

"I do too, sweetheart, but they just don't understand him, and it scares them."

"But why? Why would they be afraid of Elijah? He wouldn't hurt anybody."

"People are sometimes afraid of the things they don't understand, and he's so hard to understand." Her soothing tone was coupled with her fingertips moving through her daughter's hair.

Leah continued her trek, careful not to stray from the fluorescent stones that zigzagged toward the burning span.

———

I turned several times to watch Kathleen sleep, wanting to lay beside her and pick up where we'd left off. But time was tight, so I pieced together what I was able to, until I couldn't keep my eyes open any longer.

After saving the file on a flash drive, I closed the computer and crashed on the bed, resulting in an arm around me. "Are you done?"

"Just with the groundwork, but don't worry, I have an offering for the King."

"Such a loyal subject," she whispered. "What time is it?"

"About four."

"You should sleep. You can sleep on the way to the airport too."

Two hours later, I felt like I'd just closed my eyes.

"Wake up, David." With a hand on my shoulder, Kathleen stood beside the bed. "Thanks for letting me sleep. I didn't realize how exhausted I was. But you need to get up and get packed."

"A few more minutes," I mumbled and rolled over.

"Sure. You wanna miss your flight? No problem."

With that, I sat up, stretched, and wondered how I'd ever make it through the day.

The recognition dinner was important to my career, but I felt guilty for leaving. Some progress had been made, but despite the few phrases I was able to extract, there were still steps to be taken before I'd have anything conclusive.

"I have a few patients to check on, and need to have Dr. Young assign someone to cover me. So, I'll meet you here in about an hour."

"Wait," I said with a yawn, and pointed to the nightstand. "Will you give that flash drive to the King for me?"

"Of course," she said, then leaned over to kiss me.

Dreading the flight and needing rest, I stayed in bed for several minutes before somehow managing to put my feet on the floor and make it into the shower.

Escorted by his driver, an old man entered the main lobby. The guard held the door open, and a cold wind blew through the entry.

Dressed in a dark Italian suit, over which was an equally expensive overcoat, he walked in as though he owned the place—and in some ways, he did.

Like a maitre d' studying table settings, his alert eyes, deeply etched with lines of age, examined the hospital as he looked from corner to corner. The years had taken a toll on his posture, but he commanded respect and sustained an unyielding presence.

"Shall I wait in the car, Sir?" the driver asked, to which the man merely nodded his approval.

"Ian Young," his voice was wry. "I'm here to see Doctor Young."

"Yes. This way," the guard said, extending a helping hand, which the elder ignored as he followed with his walking cane. "He's here for Dr. Young," he spoke through the administrative window.

The receptionist peered through, then quickly picked up the phone. She'd seen this man before.

"Dr. Young, Joseph Goforth is here."

What's he doing here? He thought, then responded, "Yes, please bring him in."

She pointed toward the hallway and began to speak,

but was interrupted. "I *know* where it is. Just tell him I'm here." Joseph began walking down the corridor, and a few steps from the door, he was greeted by Dr. Young.

"Joseph, good to see you." He placed a hand on his shoulder and ushered him in. "Hold my calls," he instructed his secretary before they entered his lavish office.

After a moment of silence, during which the old man seated himself, Ian asked, "So, what can I do for you, Joseph?"

"I've come for my grandson," he responded.

"But..."

"But *nothing*," he frowned."We have an arrangement, or have you forgotten?" Reaching into his overcoat, he pulled out a cigar, which Dr. Young promptly lit for him.

"Leah hasn't improved. Her condition's still quite critical." His tone and overall demeanor were much different than when he addressed his subordinates. With a hint of humility, "We're trying several strategies..." he added.

"So that's what you call it? Strategies?" Joseph grinned. "Keep her as long as you have to. I want my grandson."

"The two of them shouldn't be separated. We discussed this..." Dr. Young tried to reason with him, but was interrupted.

"I don't care." Raising a pale shaky hand, he drew from the cigar and blew smoke into the air. "We both know I don't have long, Ian. Days are precious now. And I've allowed all of your tests, even stood for your quack dream expert from out west. But I'm sure as hell not getting any younger and I want to *know* my grandson before I die."

"Yes, I understand, but, respectfully, the two shouldn't be separated. And Leah will need rehabilitation."

"We have a deal." He was adamant.

"Yes, but that deal is that *both* twins are to be released when she recovers. I can't allow..."

"Can't *allow*?" Joseph glared. "Who do you think butters your bread, Doctor? Or perhaps I should address the Board of Directors regarding our..."

This time it was Ian who interrupted. "That won't be necessary. Just be reasonable. Give us two weeks." Hoping the offer would be accepted, he finished, "If within two weeks she hasn't awakened, I'll arrange Elijah's release."

"I'll give you one," Joseph answered. "And you should be damned glad I'm giving you that."

It was final. In one week, regardless of the condition of his twin, Elijah Goforth was to leave Meadowsview with a grandfather he'd never known.

Chapter 14 – Departure

The dark side of Nevaeh was perplexing, and though she knew she was safe, the landscape wasn't what Leah expected.

Emily said I'll be fine as long as I keep my conviction... faith.

"I have faith," she whispered, then repeated louder, "I have faith." *And nothing here can hurt me...*

She hesitated when she felt the heat of the flames.

"Give us this day, our daily bread..." She trusted the scriptures, which she understood far better than her father. While Jacob twisted and manipulated the words to intimidate and chastise, she knew them to be lessons of divination. "And forgive us our trespasses..."

With each step the heat grew more intense. Burning. Blistering. She stayed on the stones, stopping when it became unbearable.

It's so hot—but it can't burn me. And I've come too far to turn back.

Knowing her fate was beyond Erif Crossing, she drew several deep breaths, and then stepped barefooted into the flames that greedily consumed the wooden structure.

———

"I must say, I'm a bit disappointed," Dr. Young began. "I expected a little more."

Surprised by his tone, "This is only his preliminary report," Kathleen replied. "He'll send the rest when..."

"Ah, yes, when he gets back to Los Angeles," he interrupted. "Is he incapable of following even the simplest direction? I asked for a full report, not scrambled words in indiscernible columns." He pointed to the screen. "How the hell am I to make any sense of this? 'Root Thought, Derivative A, Associative Complex.' It might just as well be written in Swahili. No directions. No key. Nothing. Like I'm supposed to be some kind of mind reader."

"He said he'll work on it during his flight, and I know he's good for it."

"Good for it, huh? He's leaving at a time that makes me question whether or not he's 'good' for it." Pressing an intercom button, "Get Jon in here," he commanded, then faced her. "We're going with an alternate plan."

"Just like that? Before giving him a chance? Let David do what he's capable of doing, what we brought him here to do."

"We? As I recall it was *you* who insisted on calling him. I even told you I thought it was a bad idea, and would take too much time—time we don't have." Under the gun after Joseph Goforth's unexpected demand for his grandson, he paused. "Dr. Svelgaard and I have discussed this option in great depth, and though it's not my preferred approach, at least it's a plan." He removed the flash drive from its port. "With due respect to Dr. Weston, his untimely departure leaves me little choice but to follow my gut, and right now my gut's telling me to trust Jon. He's a brilliant surgeon."

"What's the other plan?" Kathleen's skin grew tight. "You haven't even given him a chance. For God's sake, Ian, give him some time. I *know* David, and I know he won't let us down."

"Let *you* down? Isn't that what you mean?" Placing the device in her hand, he continued. "David's not reliable. He's out of touch, and quite frankly, out of his league."

"Out of his league? Are you completely unaware of his work?"

"Apparently I don't keep up with him as closely as you." The garish tone continued. "He had a choice, and he chose Los Angeles."

"He 'chose' to attend an important career function, something that was planned well before now and can't be rescheduled." She briefly wondered if David would really return, but despite too many unanswered messages, she knew the answer. "And he'll be back next week."

"Is that right? Next week? And you don't question his degree of commitment to this case? C'mon dear, wake up and smell the coffee."

"I'll talk to him on the way to Albany, and try to have

him break it down a little more."

"You just don't get it, do you? This is more about *when* he's leaving than the results of his test. And the decision's been made."

"What decision? And why the sudden rush?" She tried to stay calm, but was seething, and Ian could tell.

"When every minute can affect her recovery, I have to consider all options, and I've decided not to delay the procedure. It's already scheduled."

"What procedure? What's this 'option' you've chosen without even consulting with me?" This time she waited for an answer.

"Exploratory surgery," he replied. "Jon said there's something..."

"What? You've gotta be kidding! And it's already scheduled?" Suddenly she felt like everything was unraveling. "I'm sorry he didn't provide you with the key. But even if he had, you've always had a knack for doing whatever Jon suggests."

"Watch yourself, Dr. Scott. I'm the one who makes the decisions here, and don't forget it."

"As her primary doctor, I expect to approve or deny any..."

"Any *what,* decisions of your superior? Don't blame me because your celebrity boyfriend couldn't hasten his findings."

"He was up all night working on this." She raised her left hand, showing him the thumb drive. "Does that mean anything to you? Or did you and Jon discuss that too?"

"Don't think for a moment that my friendship with your father entitles you to insubordination. David will be gone for days, and I'm not convinced his results are even worth waiting for."

With fiery eyes she pounded her fists, then pushed several pages and items from the desktop to the floor. "Insubordination? You have the nerve to approve an invasive surgery without my knowledge, and accuse me of insubordination?"

"You're out of line, Doctor."

"Oh, you haven't *seen* out of line yet. I swear to God, Ian—Doctor Young—if you or Jon lay one hand on that girl, I'll show you out of line!"

After slamming the door, she confronted Jon in the hallway. "No doubt surgery was *your* idea?" She pushed his chest. "Well you'd better come up with another plan. Do you hear me? If you so much as *breathe* on Leah, *you'll* be the one needing exploratory surgery."

To the stunned stares of several staff members who watched in disbelief, Kathleen quick-stepped across the marble floor to the elevator. Inside, she stared at her reflection before bursting into tears.

― ― ―

"Leeeaaaahhhh," the faint voice was just beyond the gathering crackle of flames fully surrounding her.

"Leeeaaaahhhh," she heard it again and tensely stopped to the call of her father.

"No!" she shouted. "Yea, though I walk through the valley of..."

"I know you're there. I can see you," he tormented.

She continued the verse, only louder, attempting to drown out his summons. "The shadow of death!"

"You can't hide from me, for I am the Deacon."

"I pity you!" Her thoughts grew angry, but fearful of going backwards, she tried to dismiss them. "I shall fear no evil!" She boldly continued, "Not even *you* father!" This was *her* dream, or nightmare—whatever it was, it was hers—and the beguiling Jacob was not welcome. "I shall fear no evil, and you can't hurt me here, so *go.* Go to hell, where you belong!" With conviction, firm and deliberate, she shouted louder, "Leave me alone!"

I didn't go backwards... But I do pity him, so it's not a lie...

She'd unknowingly confronted her greatest fear, and with her faith clearly intact, Leah stepped through the fire, unscathed by the heat of the flames.

Thrown out. Expelled. Jacob was banished from her dream and would haunt her no more.

"After the fiery bridge you'll climb to the peak of Mount Epoh Sevil." Emily had pointed to the mountain that now towered before Leah. *"Then you'll cross the middle bridge to Lanrete Efil."*

After several steps she turned to look back.

The glow of red, yellow, and blue flames swept upward and were mirrored in the water below the bridge. Like cellophane in a pool of darkness, the fire danced in the ebb and flow of the slow current.

Kathleen's silence grew more unbearable with each mile-marker.

I looked through the windshield, feeling like I was

betraying her by leaving. Not knowing what to say, or if I should say anything at all, I really didn't want to leave. Not now. The timing couldn't be worse.

Beside me, Kathleen's avoidance of eye contact, and complete silence, said everything.

"Could you maybe just yell at me, or slap me or something?" I couldn't take it anymore. "I know it's a bad time. I know I'm leaving at a bad time, but if I miss this dinner I'll lose my agent, plus the respect of several people who already question my judgment."

"And we wouldn't want *that* to happen, would we?" Her irony was like a loaded gun pressed against my temple, and I waited for her to pull the trigger, which she did. "What about the twins? *My* colleagues? Their opinion? Me? Jesus, what about *me*?" Her tone was gravely vulnerable.

"I'll be back as soon as I can. I'll take a red-eye tomorrow night if you want."

"But what do *you* want?" She glanced at me with searching eyes.

"I want you, if that's what you mean?"

My answer surprised us both.

"Are you sure? I mean, if you need time..." Her eyes swelled up with tears as she offered a conciliatory smile. "I don't wanna twist your arm, ya know?"

"I want you."

"But are you sure?" she said nervously. "I mean, let's face it, you don't have a very good track record, so you'll have to excuse me for not taking anything for granted."

"I can't argue with that," I said, knowing there was basis for her doubt. "All I know," I grappled for just the right words. "All I know is that I will come back, and we'll discuss everything."

Unspoken words sometimes wound as deeply as those said in haste. I wanted to say it, but I didn't. The truth was, I'd always loved her—enough to keep her at a safe distance, away from the minefields around me.

"But if a butterfly flaps its wings in LA, will you still be back?" The question had multiple meanings.

"Tell ya what," I said. "I'll be back if one flaps its wings *anywhere*."

When we reached the terminal, she pulled to the curb and turned the ignition off. "Have a good flight, and call me when you get there—use that phone for a change." She moved her knees to the console between us, giving me a good view of her smooth legs.

"You're not nice," I grinned.

"Really? You thought I was pretty nice this morning."

After a tenuous kiss, I got out and took my bag from the back seat. Hesitating, I faced her.

"I know," she said. "I've always known. Just call me when you get there. Okay?"

I nodded.

After going through security, I went directly to my gate, and within a few minutes an announcement came over the public address. "Flight 1720 to Los Angeles now boarding."

Bags in hand, I took a place in line, not looking forward to the several hours I'd spend en route home.

A few steps away from the ticket-taker, a surge went through me. *The train bridge, David*. It was Lani, predictably repeating the phrase she'd said time and again over the past several days, but with a disturbing degree of urgency this time.

"Are you okay, Sir?" a concerned attendant asked as she took the pass from my shaking hand.

"Yes, fine," I nodded and managed a smile as I continued to board.

Halfway across the ramp I suddenly felt completely disoriented. *Turn around,* she whispered.

Stopping, to the intrusive looks of other passengers, I went back into the terminal and approached the counter.

"May I help you?"

"Yes, I need a flight to Huntington."

She struck a few keys. "There's a connecting flight in Cincinnati with a fifty-four minute layover. Is that okay?"

Fate was taking me to West Virginia, so I nodded and made the switch.

Another day, another wait, another flight. The mundane sequence had accounted for many hours of my life, but this time was different.

It was rare for me to give anything more of myself than what was required, and in my pursuit of success I'd forgotten, or merely left many things along the way. On another day I would have gone home to Los Angeles and the award dinner, but not this day.

While trying to appear composed, I nervously recounted the images and voices of the past week. Maybe I was losing my mind, but I took a seat facing the tarmac and waited for the boarding call. Alert, perplexed, I yielded to the ethereal child compelling me to take a life-changing detour.

When we arrived at the Tri-State terminal—which seemed almost abandoned compared to Albany and Cincinnati—the pace was much slower.

"What listing please?" the operator asked.

"Huntington Hills Hospital, Psychology Department."

"Would you like me to connect you?"

"Please."

The phone rang twice. "Psychology Department."

"Hello, is Dr. Lambert in?"

"One moment please."

"Dr. Lambert's office," another woman answered. "May I ask who's calling?"

"This is David Weston, and it's regarding the Goforth twins."

"Please hold." She cuffed the receiver with the palm of her hand, and a third voice was soon on the line.

"Hello, this is Dr. Lambert."

"Dr. Lambert, this is David Weston."

"The psychologist?"

"Yes..."

"What can I do for you, Dr. Weston?"

"I'm in Huntington, and would like to meet with you. Right away, if possible."

"And this is about the Goforth children?"

"Yes. I'm sorry for not calling in advance."

"When can you be here?" Her tone had the same

strange sense of urgency I'd felt since changing flights. "I have a meeting this afternoon. Can you be here by two?"

I looked at my watch. It was one-seventeen. "Sure, I think so."

"Okay, I'll see you then. Just come to the third floor."

After trying to decipher directions from a rental-car rep, I bought a map and drove to the northern outskirts of town.

Shortly after two, I parked and made my way to the lobby.

Considerably smaller than Meadowsview, the hospital was in need of a few repairs, the most obvious being the well worn carpet that was stained and fraying.

I stepped out of the elevator on the third floor, and was surprised to find a barred door, resembling a jail cell, complete with a security guard who immediately asked for identification.

"And the reason for your visit, Mr. Weston?"

"I'm meeting with Dr. Lambert," I answered, to which he handed my license back to me and pressed a button that unlocked the door.

"Everything out of your pockets," he said and placed a plastic tray on the table beside me. He then pressed another button, unlocking the inner door. "Straight down this hallway. Her secretary will be right with you."

Walking alertly through Huntington Hill's psychiatric ward, I avoided eye contact with several wandering individuals. Watched by nurses and orderlies, their eyes seemed blank, even the staff, as though all of them were just going through the motions of another day.

One can't be in the midst of people in that condition without being grateful for his own. *What the hell*, I thought about being a few minutes late—at least I was there.

"Are you Dr. Weston?" A staff member in a tight-fitting skirt approached from the other side of the hallway.

"Yes."

"This way please. I'm Dr. Lambert's assistant, Caroline." I loved the sweet southern accent, it was one of my many weaknesses. "Dr. Lambert says you're a real piece of work," she added.

"Oh she does, does she?"

I followed her to the end of the hall, where she entered her code on a keypad that unlocked a metal door. She then led me through a narrow walkway where several clerks curiously turned as we ambled between their cubicles.

In a corner office that had a beautiful view of the Cabell County autumn, Caroline introduced us. "Dr. Weston, Dr. Lambert."

She was much younger than I'd imagined. An attractive black woman, her straight dark hair had red streaks that complemented her warm smile.

"Helen," she said, shaking my hand with an incisive demeanor. "How is Leah?"

"Still asleep."

Decorated with autumn leaves and small ceramic pumpkins, her office reminded me of Annie's. Vibrant.

Uplifting.

A collage on the wall near her desk caught my attention, and with a closer look, two of the photos stood out...

The first was of Leah, smiling like any ordinary girl, but with dark, penetrating eyes—much like Lani's.

And the other picture was of Elijah, who, as always, was drawing.

"So," she said. "Please, have a seat."

Her assistant politely returned to her own desk, and Helen faced me. "She's gifted."

"Yeah, I got that from your reports. But what I'm not clear about is what caused the coma, and how to..." I hesitated.

"How to bring her out?"

"Well, yes." I felt shallow for stating the obvious.

"We're *all* wondering about that, Dr. Weston."

"David. Please call me David."

"She has to 'want' to wake up," she said matter-of-factly. "She needs to have reason to return to life. With her history of abuse, her mother's suicide..."

"Wait. Suicide?"

"I thought you read my reports?"

"I knew she died, but..."

"Two days after the twins were admitted, Naomi supposedly took her own life. At least, that's the 'official' line..."

"Sounds like you have doubts," I said.

"I met her. Kind. Attentive. She loved the twins, and wouldn't do that to them. Not in a million years."

Chapter 15 - Epoh Sevil

Mount Epoh Sevil towered above, its silhouette slowly revealed in the morning sunlight. But light never touched the dark valley from which Leah had come.

Several stones on the north bank led to narrow steps carved into the mountainside.

Placing her right foot on the first step, she arched her neck to see the very summit. *Epoh Sevil,* she thought. *Epoh... Hope. Hope Lives...* She remembered Naomi saying to meet her 'Where hope lives.'

Where hope lives is Epoh Sevil... "I'm coming," she said as tears started to streak down her soot-covered cheeks. "I'm coming, mommy..."

―――――

Elijah stared at the foliage behind Meadowsview. Leah's rejection had left him hurt and confused, even his drawing seemed unimportant. More alone than ever, he knew that he wasn't welcome in her dream. Huddled near the window frame, he watched the falling leaves swirl to the ground.

"Are you ready for our meeting?" Annie stepped inside.

Tense, he moved into a defensive position.

"Elijah?" she asked, concerned by his behavior. She then noticed that there was no rendering on the table. "Elijah, why aren't you drawing?"

"She doesn't want me to." He continued facing the window.

"Who?"

"Leah," he answered, and with an unusual show of emotion, added, "She doesn't want me there, and she won't come back."

Annie stood quietly watching for a moment, not knowing how to respond. Finally, she asked, "Did she tell you that?"

"Yes," he answered, looking through the corners of his eyes. "She told me to go away."

In the several days since their arrival he'd never said as much. Always before, it was a word or two here and there, followed by periods of silence. Annie was stunned by his sudden change and revelations.

"Where *is* your sister?" she asked, unprepared for his response.

"Heaven." His spasms briefly stopped as he turned to her with distant eyes.

— — —

The terrain leveled off for several paces, and Leah rested. Behind her, Erif Crossing continued to burn. Red and blue flames swept upward, the only light in the desolate valley she'd come through.

Further south, the hillside was covered with fields of heather that projected a violet glow on the clouds above.

And beyond that, on the very southern horizon, the faint outline of the fortress showed her how far she'd come—and how far away she was from her friends.

I wish Scarecrow could have come with me.

Turning back, she again faced the summit where she was convinced she would be reunited with Naomi.

———

"Elijah," Annie asked. "Can you talk to your sister?"

He began slowly rocking back and forth, and then nervously answered, "No. Not anymore."

Annie gripped her glasses. "Why not anymore?" Regardless of whether or not he continued, to her this was a breakthrough session. But he again surprised her.

"She won't let me." He rocked faster, beside himself with frustration.

Seeing his edgy, vulnerable state, she attempted to revert his attention back to what calmed him the most. "Can we look at your drawings?"

He stopped moving. With the weight of the world on his shoulders, he again looked through the corners of his eyes.

"Yes," he finally answered and turned gravely back to

the glass.

"I hate to interrupt, but if I was married to that man I'd probably kill myself too," Caroline said. "Or hang him from the highest tree," she brashly finished.

Embarrassed by her assistant's outspokenness, Helen raised an eyebrow and then asked directly, "So what can I really help you with?"

Grinning, I felt foolish. "Do you know where any coal bridges are?"

"Coal bridges?"

"Well, yeah, like the kind coal trains use."

"I know of a few north of here, but why?"

"I'm looking for a specific bridge. It crosses a deep ravine and there are tunnels through the mountains on either side."

Her assistant answered. "Why, they all do that, silly." Batting her eyes and turning back to her desk, she bluntly finished. "Maybe you should start with the one Naomi Goforth jumped off."

"Caroline," Dr. Lambert reprimanded, "Is that report done?"

"No ma'am," she answered. "I'll just..." She spun back to her desk, trying to appear professional, but smiling.

"Is that true? Naomi jumped from a bridge?" My mind raced a hundred miles an hour... *Elijah's bridge?*

"Jumped. Fell..." she answered. "The sheriff's report says suicide, but some aren't so sure."

"And you? What do you think?"

"I think they were quick to reach their conclusion."

— — —

Staggering the final steps to the summit, Leah fell onto the grassy mountaintop. Exhausted from the long climb to the peak of Epoh Sevil, she lay prone, awaiting the arrival of Naomi, and thinking of her brother. *God, take care of Elijah.*

"Leahhhh!" Naomi's voice echoed through Nevaeh. Climbing a similar, but shorter stairway on the other side of the mountain, she skipped steps at the sight of her little girl.

"Where were you?" Leah asked, springing to her feet with tears streaking her sullied skin.

"Here," Naomi answered as she reached the crest. "I've been here, and I *am* here!" She opened her arms, drawing her daughter into the sanctuary that she alone could provide.

Tightly clutching her mother's robe, Leah wept uncontrollably, causing Naomi to also cry as she held her tightly in her arms.

Wiping her damp cheeks, "This is *really* Heaven?" Leah asked.

"Yes, this is a part of Heaven!"

"But..." Leah looked toward the middle bridge. "Why are there more bridges?"

"It's okay." Naomi lightly stroked her daughter's dark hair. "You'll understand when you get there. But we don't have much time. You have to go on, and I have to go back." She looked into the lush valley where herds of strangely colored horses grazed.

"Why? Why do you have to go back?"

"For now, I can go no further in Nevaeh. The valley below is where I may spend eternity." Naomi smiled contentedly, finding no reason to explain the sins which kept her from attaining a higher level of ascent. "But here on Epoh Sevil, hope *does* live. So tell me. Tell me, child. What do you hope for?"

Looking into the valley, Leah hesitated. Finally, she answered. "I hope Elijah gets to ride on a train."

"But what do you want for *you*?"

Leah was quiet. What she wanted most, was for Naomi to return to them, but she knew that was no longer an option.

"I want to stay here with you." She gazed curiously into the valley. "I could stay here!" She held her mother tight, wanting to remain with her in the lush pastures below.

"But you can't stay here, Leah."

"But why not? You asked what I hope, and I want to stay here. I don't wanna go back, and I don't wanna go on. I just wanna stay here with you."

"I'm sorry. I know it's hard to understand, but I have no say. I don't make the decisions here. Besides, what you find at the next level will change your mind."

"But if I keep going, can I still be with you?"

"I'll always be there, no matter where you go."

"But you don't talk to me anymore. And I can't see you. So how can I know when you're there?"

"I'm always there, child. Can you see the wind?"

"No, of course not."

"So how do you know it's there? If you can't see it, it

doesn't exist?"

"I understand," Leah said. "But I don't feel you like I feel the wind. You left us. You left me and Elijah alone." She looked across the Span of Epoh Sevil, the bridge between the two highest peaks of Nevaeh.

With time fading and her daughter's fate beyond the next crossing, Naomi asked again. "What do you wish for you, baby?"

"I don't know," Leah answered, uncertainty written in her dark eyes. "I wish Elijah was safe too. Maybe I shouldn't have left him alone." She stared contritely at her mother. "You already did that to *both* of us."

Time to go, David. This time Lani's voice was as clear as a bell over the public address system.

"I know! I know!" I responded out loud, to the surprise and uncertain stares of the psychiatrist and her assistant.

"Are you okay, Doctor?" Helen frowned with concern.

"Didn't you hear that?" I asked, drawing deep breaths and shaking.

"Hear what?"

Of course they didn't hear. "Never mind." I tried to collect myself.

"Maybe you should just check into a motel and have a good night's rest," Caroline suggested.

"You probably *should* get some rest," Helen agreed.

But the frequent and now public appearances by Lani had convinced me that time was running out.

"Maybe I will," I lied, with no intention of doing

anything but visiting the bridge in Elijah's drawing. Embarrassed, and having lost all credibility, I just wanted out of there. "So exactly where is this bridge?"

"It's up the road, about thirty minutes north." Caroline winked, to her supervisor's disapproving gaze.

"Perhaps you really should unwind first?" Helen faced me. "You're pale and shaking." She looked at my trembling hands. "And those roads are narrow and dangerous."

Attempting to regain her confidence, "I'm fine," I said. "Sometimes I just think out loud."

Caroline eagerly printed out a map page, wanting to be of any assistance at all, as Dr. Lambert continued trying to dissuade me.

"You're very close to this," Helen said. And I knew what she meant. "You could even crash here in the hospital," she made a last attempt to keep me from leaving.

I smiled, but politely declined. "I appreciate the offer, but I really should be going."

"Well, okay. Good luck, Dr. Weston. I mean, David." She stepped between me and the door, peculiarly tightening her grip as we shook hands. "But will you please call me if you have any problems?" She handed me her card, and a strange surge went through me as I realized that Helen too was somehow a part of the Goforth Situation.

"Of course." I placed her card in my shirt-pocket along with the map her assistant had given me. Releasing her hand, I again followed Caroline through the hallway of wandering souls.

"Well, dahlin', if you change your mind, I do know of a couple motels." She smiled provocatively.

I bet you do. With an approving review of her high-heels, smooth legs, and form-fitting sweater, I acknowledged that she was a looker, but silently declined. On another day I might've stayed, but not this day. Something was different—me. Hundreds of miles away, a chapter of my life had ended, and a new one started. I was changed, and Kathleen was the reason. She was one of those forces of nature I'd never understand.

― ― ―

"Why?" Leah asked, not even trying to conceal her heartbreak.

"Why?" Naomi responded. "Why what?"

"Why did you leave us? I had the telling. I saw you jump."

"No!" Naomi gasped. "I didn't jump!"

"But I *saw*!"

"There's no time now, but as you cross this bridge you'll see. Here, there are only you and your memories." She held her daughter tightly. "No tests, no obstacles, just you. And on the other side are angels with tambourines and harps. Some even have wings!" Naomi stared at the crossing, wondering if she would ever have her own wings. And after a final embrace, she began back down the steps carved into the mountainside. "Faith, baby." She looked over her shoulder. "Have faith."

There was no time to lose or reason to remain. Before her, Leah could see no end to the gently swaying link between Mount Epoh Sevil and Lanrete Efil. *I have to hurry... I have to get there before sunset!* Wondering when she would see her mother again, she started across the span, toward the promise of eternity. *I trust in God. I do trust in You.* Resolute, she continued, each step bringing her closer to destiny.

When we reached the security gate, Caroline politely shook my hand then smiled one last time before turning around. The guard buzzed me in and I collected my things.

In the car, I rested my head on the steering wheel, feeling like a complete idiot for my outburst in the hospital. Since my return from Lauani, my visions had been inconsistent. Sometimes I'd go for weeks without seeing her, then I'd see her everyday. But she was appearing more frequently now, and with galvanized determination.

For several minutes, I sat there in the rental car, staring directly at the ER entrance. I finally put the key in the ignition and looked in the rearview mirror.

Lani's reflection stared back at me. "Hi David," she said.

I took a quick breath, and turned around. She was more real than any time before, and was looking directly at me.

"Sad, isn't it?" she said. "What happened to Leah is so sad." Shy. Soft-spoken. Sincere. She had a sense of elegance, natural beauty, innocence. And her dark eyes were like portals into her soul. Penetrating. Paralyzing.

"Yes," I finally answered.

"Drive," she instructed, to which I released the brake and put the car in reverse.

Her voice then came from the passenger seat. "I'll show you the way." She was suddenly sitting beside me.

"Jesus," I said, as she played with the visor. "And you know the way to the bridge?"

"Yes," she answered, then pointed at two women in a third floor window, watching us—or me.

"Can they see you?"

"No. Sometimes even you can't see me."

Great. I waved goodbye to Helen and Caroline. *They must really think I'm crazy... Maybe they're right.*

"No. You're not crazy." She turned on the radio. Startled, she jumped, then stared with the same inquisitive eyes I'd seen before—in another place, another time.

Giggling, she turned the dial until coming to a song with a slow beat. "Drive," she said, pointing north. "Go that way."

I'd given up on finding forgiveness, but looking over my shoulder, it seemed forgiveness had somehow found me.

Chapter 16 - The Seventh Bridge

I could have been on my way home, but was instead in the hills of West Virginia.

Here, my privileged life, doctorate, lectures, none of that mattered. In this strange land *I* was the stranger, an uninvited blight on the not-so-delicate balance of life.

Lani had pointed to each turn along the way, and I wasn't surprised when we turned onto a gravel road that ended at a deep canyon.

To the left, an old bridge—Elijah's bridge—stretched across the divide.

Walking to the edge, the muffled echoes of howling dogs defined the depth of the gorge, which was easily more than two hundred feet.

In the late afternoon light the entire scene was like nothing I'd ever seen. The bridge seemed to perfectly suit the landscape, as though they were melded into one, giving it a timeless, eerie presence.

Elijah's drawing was so precise that I felt like I'd seen it in a postcard. But there was a cold anticipation that further chilled the late October air.

"This way," Lani said softly, and then louder. "David, this way." She began down the thin path snaking the edge of the ravine. "Come. Don't be afraid. I know the way."

For a long time, as far back as the island, she had been leading me here. Lani seemed to have always known the way to Elijah's bridge, just as she'd known my plagued memories, visions, guilt—everything that had brought me to this moment and this place.

"Hurry," she said, "follow me."

She disappeared when a voice came from the woods.

"I don't believe I know you." Tall, with broad shoulders, he stood only steps away. "I don't think I know you, stranger."

"David Weston," I said, facing Elijah's bridge. "That's some sight, isn't it?" I tried to look like a lost tourist. "You don't see *that* everyday."

Staring directly at me, his gray eyes were devoid of emotion. "You're not from around here."

"No, I'm..."

"What you *are* is on private property, Mr. Weston." He grinned. "I suggest you just turn yourself around and get off my land."

"I understand," I said. "I apologize. I'll just go back to my car." I nodded in that direction. "Sorry to disturb you."

Leaving, I looked over my shoulder twice.

His stare—probing, calculating—made me consider

driving back to Huntington and going home, but Lani had different plans.

"He's gone," she said.

I turned to see him walking up the hillside, then back to the path, where Lani stood in the middle of the trail.

"What are you doing? Where are you going? You can't stop now. No. You have to *finish* this."

"Finish *what?* You're not even real." I laughed at my delusion, walking through her as though she was nothing more than a vapor.

I told myself she wasn't really there, that she was merely a creation of my guilt-ridden conscience, but she appeared again, directly ahead of me.

"If I'm not real, how did you get here? Did you even *look* at that map?" She smiled. "Maybe you just 'wished' yourself here or 'guessed' your way to this canyon. Was *that* it? Huh?"

With no answer, I stopped. Maybe I *was* crazy, but the map was still folded in my shirt pocket, where it had been since Caroline handed it to me. There was no denying that Lani's directions had led me there, just as she'd led me to West Virginia.

"He's gone now. Follow me," she urged. "Don't leave this unfinished."

I looked toward the car, then turned back to the bridge. "Come on," she said, her dark eyes reflecting the faint glow of dusk.

We followed the trail to a service-access ladder leading up to the bridge. Perhaps twenty feet high, Lani had scaled it and was stepping onto the terrain above as I began up the first rusty steps. Staring first at me, she then gazed down the length of the tracks. "This is what you've been looking for."

I was there when she drew her last breath, and was reduced to ashes in that far away lagoon, but she never really went away. She was with me. She remained.

"Come." She pointed to the other side. "Come cross Elijah's Bridge."

I reached the top step and pulled myself up as her colorful island skirt blew in the wind.

"Beautiful, isn't it?" She held her hands above her head as evening shadows filled the canyon.

"Yes," I answered, my eyes swollen with tears as I remembered her running across the white sands of Lauani with a balloon in her hand. If she was of my own conjuring, I'd left no facet of the illusion untouched. She stood before me, a year older and speaking perfect English.

"You're a good man, David," she said, then lowered her arms. "And I forgave you a long time ago. But now you need to forgive yourself."

Standing between the rails I faced her and wondered what solace, if any, I might find in being there.

Muffled in the wind, the howls were more distant, as I paused for a moment and walked past her.

When I turned to look back, she was gone.

Alone on Elijah's bridge, I knew it was too late to consider what I was doing there. *But why am I here?*

— — —

Leah began across the span, stopping when she noticed her own shadow in the valley below.

"The second level is between the summits, and crosses the Golden Valley." Emily had placed her entire palm on the parchment to show how long the span was. "You can't fall from this bridge, and nothing there can hurt you."

Gazing into the great valley that her mother said was where some angels wait for their wings, she watched the painted ponies graze below.

From beneath the bridge came the rhythmic clatter of a single sprinting horse. Looking down, Leah saw her mother riding a blue Appaloosa with red spots.

"Faith, baby!" she shouted, running the animal to the others, who looked alertly toward the clamor.

Waving to her mother, Leah saw joy and content that made leaving even harder. But the distant peak called, and she continued to cross the rope and wood bridge, confused, frightened, and more alone than ever.

At first they were glimpses of infancy—very dim, almost transparent, and easily unnoticed. Like faintly painted window panes, they hovered toward her and then passed. But with every step they became more vivid, as though the closer she came to the present, the more real the images were. Her earliest memories lasted only a few steps, but one-by-one Leah recounted the days, like a chronological slide-show of her life.

A salvo of memories besieged her as she quickened the pace across the Span of Epoh Sevil.

Before long, her first six years had flown by, but then, drawn to a particular image, she hesitated.

Looking intently at the panel, she caused the

remembrance to hover in front of her...

Elijah, with her encouragement, had drawn on the wall of their bedroom, and when Jacob came home he was not pleased.

"No Daddy!" Leah stepped between him and her twin. "He didn't do it!"

"*You* did this?" the preacher asked.

"Yes," she lied sweetly. "*I* did this."

"Show me!" Jacob hastily handed her a crayon and page he tore from a spiral notebook. "Show me!" he demanded.

Leah knew then that she was a sinner, as the Reverend always reminded her.

Struggling in her attempt to match Elijah's talent, *I wish I could draw like you,* she thought.

"Sinful, lying child!" Jacob led her to the dining room, where he pulled out the familiar chair.

Having drawn her father's anger away from her brother, *Go Elijah, go!* she thought. Knowing he couldn't stand on the chair for very long, she often took his place.

He stumbled quickly to his bed, and covered his eyes before peering into the other room, where his twin accepted his punishment.

I could have done it, ya know?

I know, she answered, attempting to console him. *You can take the blame for me next time.*

She had always protected him. From an early age, she understood not only the difficulty of his struggles, but the significance of his accomplishments. Selfless, and without regret, she knew that Elijah was graced in other ways.

Recollections of her life—her sacrifice, loyalty, humility, and pain—were all assembled in an onslaught of images that flew past on either side.

Most of the memories were trivial, and went by quickly, but some were captivating, causing her to stop several times.

When she could see the other side, she lingered only on the visions that made her smile, holding them briefly before letting them pass.

But the memories of her last days were frightening, making the final steps the hardest.

Paralyzed, she viewed one from a new angle.

Reliving the moment she foresaw her mother's leap, she wanted to step into the peaceful grass before her, but didn't. With only two steps between her and sanctuary, she had to know what happened.

Why would she leave us? We needed her. Why would she leave me and Elijah? And why would she... Staring wide-eyed into the panel, she took a step backwards when the frame revealed someone behind Naomi on the bridge.

She tried to ignore the image and take the final steps to the peak, but couldn't. Instead, Leah faced the truth for the first time.

———

Starting her shift, Rebecca settled into her chair.

Having gone through her checklist more thoroughly than ever, she couldn't turn her gaze away from Leah.

The patient's log was the only thing on the table that usually held several magazines and a novel.

Impacted by the events of the previous night, she picked it up and began looking for accounts of the incident, but found none. There were no references to the power outage, and none about the bizarre occurrences of the night before.

She turned frequently to the girl she'd seen open her eyes only hours ago, wondering why there was no mention of the test.

Confused, she was lost in thought when an alert from the monitor stunned her.

Lunging for the intercom, "Karen, it's Leah!" she shouted. "She's flat-lining. Hurry!"

The head nurse entered, and immediately checked Leah's pulse, then ordered Rebecca to call Dr. Scott. "We need her in here *now.*"

Kathleen rushed up two flights of stairs and into Leah's room, where Karen attempted CPR.

"What happened?" she asked.

"She was fine," Rebecca responded. "Then all of the sudden her heart-rate dropped to nothing. It just stopped beating."

Kathleen reached for the defibrillator.

"Clear," Karen said, as two nurses entered the room.

"Come on, Leah," Kathleen whispered, followed by the voltage of the equipment she prayed would jump-start the girl's heart. Several seconds passed. "Again." She lowered the discs once more to Leah's chest. *God, is this déjà vu? Didn't we do this with Emily?* As she stood over Leah, her thoughts were of the girl who occupied the same room several months earlier...

His daughter was Sir Vaughn Llewellyn's heart and joy. Like him, she had hazel eyes, red hair, and a laugh that was contagious. She was mild in manner and wise beyond her years.

"What do you mean you 'don't know'? This is the fourth time in a month." With a Welsh accent, he questioned Kathleen about his daughter, who had slipped into yet another coma. "This is supposed to be the best hospital of its kind in the entire world. And you've yet to even determine *why* she keeps doing this. I want answers, not 'I don't know'."

"We're doing everything we can." Kathleen was frustrated, at a loss. Without even the vaguest reason why the apparently healthy fourteen-year-old was in and out of consciousness, she had no answers for the insistent father. "Her scans show nothing, her blood work shows nothing. There's just no clear reason for this to keep happening."

Vaughn had taken Emily to the best doctors in Europe. He was exhausted, on pins and needles, and was in Vermont as a measure of desperation.

Usually it was no more than three or four days, but this time it had been six, and he never knew if she someday wouldn't wake up at all.

"I don't mean to sound so harsh, Doctor Scott. I just..."

"There's no need to apologize. But trust me, we're doing everything we can."

She remembered his expression and the forced smile

with which he answered, "I know you are. I just don't know what I would do without her."

There are forces of nature we don't understand, and 'fate' is one of them. Sometimes it leads us, sometimes we search for it, but destiny always prevails.

Against stronger winds, I stepped from one wooden plank to the next, not knowing why I was there, what I hoped to find, or how to find it. I'd never consciously tried to summon Lani before, but I wished at that moment that she was there with me.

A quarter of the way across, I stopped, petrified by Jacob's shouts. "Who are you *really?* And what are you looking for?" His tone sent chills through me.

"Excuse me?" I responded, "You followed me up here to ask who I am?" I tried to sound fearless, but watched his every step.

Without missing a beat, he merely mimicked the local accent. "David, we don't take kindly to stranjahs heah."

He looked ten feet tall when he began across the span, but five yards away from me he stopped. "This is where my Naomi fell." His voice suddenly seemed different, almost penitent. "She loved those earrings," he added. "Her mother gave them to her."

Maybe he thought I was an investigator or journalist, but, for whatever reason, he began giving a first hand depiction of his wife's accident.

"I told her not to lean over so far, but when the feather was caught in the wind, she reached for it." Jacob was a convincing liar. "It's still down there somewhere," he finished with a somber, contrived gaze into the canyon.

"Look, I'm sorry. Sorry for crossing your property, but I don't want any trouble." He was built like a linebacker, so I figured discretion was the better part of valor.

"It's called trespassing." His response was like a playground bully during recess. "And, well, I'm sorry too, but you *found* trouble, Mr. Weston." There was an intimidating expression on his face, a morbid, self-assured smirk, as though his point of view was all that mattered. "You found *me*, Reverend Jacob Goforth, the man, the legend!" He sensed my fear and laughed. "What's wrong, David?"

"Ya know, I think I've seen enough here. Sorry for the intrusion." I walked toward him, wanting only to step past and make my way back to the rusty ladder, but he continued coming, as though he knew I was lying.

I tried to turn, but slipped on the tracks and fell to my knees. There, I noticed something shiny wedged between the rail and a wooden slat. I quickly grasped the beaded feather earring matching the one in Elijah's box.

Jacob suddenly stopped when I raised the jewelry for him to see.

"I guess it must've blown back up here," I said.

Stunned, he stared with guilt and anger.

"Well, you won't need that." He took several large steps and lunged in an attempt to take it from my hand.

Tightly clenching the earring, my body filled with adrenaline. There was no other choice but to fight.

"Go to hell!" I shouted, and threw an elbow into his side, surprising him long enough for me to regain my footing.

"You shouldn't meddle into other's business!" He was easily able to wrestle me to my back, where my head was only inches from the edge. Strong and furious, "I suppose *this* is the exact spot," he arrogantly smirked, keeping me pinned beneath him. "This is the same spot that my dear wife met *her* demise." He paused, and for a moment his eyes were compassionate, humane.

"She was beautiful, my Naomi, an angel. Wherever she was, she lit up the room." His face then went flush with rage as he pushed harder and drove a knee into my ribs. "But she lied and cheated!" His dark grin then became even more disturbing as he admitted his part in her death. "She knew the consequences. I merely suggested immediate restitution, rather than the life of an adulteress." Continuing, "I told her a life of shame would not abolish her sin." He peered off into the gorge, nodding as though his actions were justified. "And that God hath ordained that she should perish. And then, with the blessing of my touch, I sent her to atone."

A rush of pure adrenaline—as though it was being shot straight into my veins—consumed me. Naomi's death was no accident, nor was it suicide. Jacob had lured his wife to this bridge with the sole intention of sending her over the edge.

Tormented not by guilt, but by the infuriating thought of Naomi with another man, he pushed harder.

"Thou shalt *not* commit adultery!" In his twisted righteousness, he'd taken the life of the one woman who had made *him* feel alive, yet he was without remorse.

A walking dead man, Jacob Goforth was reduced to

little more than the subsequent stirs of a lifeless shadow striking the canyonside.

— — —

Catatonic, Leah watched the memory until she could no longer bear the truth. Falling forward across the last step, she allowed the memory to go by.

At the crest, she rested in the tall grass, exhausted, but knowing she had made it to the next level.

"Do you know what 'eternal' means?" The familiar voice surprised her and she rose to her feet, turning to the direction it came from.

"It means forever," she answered, and then ran the few remaining steps to the very peak, where Kris greeted her with outstretched arms.

"Yes, and that's a very long time." He held her to his chest.

"So, am I here now? Is this..."

"No child, not yet, but you're very close. Come. Walk with me." He led to a path where birds and dragonflies flew and the trees swayed to a symphony of harps and tambourines.

"But I thought I was supposed to go alone?"

"Well, there's been a change of plans." He led her to the other side of the summit.

Fearful of being denied entry into Heaven, "What change of plans?" she asked. "Emily said I have to go alone, and I went alone. She said stay on the path, so I stayed on the path, and now there's a 'change of plans'?"

They followed the stones to the northwest part of the peak, where it sloped down into to an amber field of wheat.

In the glow of dusk, they took a few more steps, then Leah suddenly stopped. "Is that...?"

"Yes," Kris answered. "It's The Rise of Lanrete Efil, the bridge to Eternity. But this is not your time, Leah."

"What? I can still make it! I'll run!" She started to sprint through the swaying field of grain.

"Wait," Kris said. "Come here, girl. Didn't Emily say to stay on the path?"

The question made her turn around."Well, how else am I supposed to get there? If I stay on the path, I won't make it before the sun disappears." She began back to the ever-present stones. Rejected. Confused.

"What if I give you a pass?" Kris smiled as she reluctantly approached.

"Pass?"

"Yes. Because this is not your time."

"I don't understand..."

"Listen. You will one day, one day a very long time from now, come back to this place. But now is not your time."

His compassionate tone was unquestionable, but Leah questioned. "Why isn't it my time?"

"Because you have many great things still to come in life."

"But..." she tried to bargain.

"But nothing," he interrupted. "Consider yourself our Angel on Earth. And God knows Earth could use a few more angels." He smiled. "And when you return, many things will be different."

"Like what?"

"You'll see."

"But why can't I just stay in the gold valley?" She nodded southerly.

"Because it's not your time."

Seeing that there was no changing his mind, she placed both feet on the next stone. "So, I can come back whenever I want?"

"Not exactly," he answered. "There are a few rules here too."

"More rules?" She frowned. "Can't we just get on with it? I'm tired of the rules. I always follow them and then I'm told there's more." Her young eyes showed her disappointment as she went on. "What am I supposed to do now? I stayed on the stones. I had faith. I came alone." Discouraged, she looked hesitantly at the stones that would now lead away from eternity.

Having come so far and feeling that Heaven was so close, she tried once more to persuade him. "I'll be a good angel, I promise. I'll work so much harder than the other angels. I'll do laundry, and clean my room, and..." Leah stopped mid-sentence, accepting the real reason she couldn't cross Lanrete Efil. "Elijah," she whispered.

"Again," Kathleen said, before trying one last time to revive Leah.

Except for the steady hum of the monitor, the room was silent.

Visibly distraught, Kathleen tried to hold herself together for the sake of her peers, but was screaming inside.

"Okay," she finally said. "I'm calling it five thirty-three."

"Five thirty-three," Karen confirmed, then handed her the log for one last entry.

"Damn it. I'm sorry." Rebecca left in tears, and the few members of the staff that had assembled outside of Leah's room began returning to their posts and patients.

It was all too familiar, and Kathleen couldn't keep from thinking of the red-haired girl who had occupied the same bed not that long ago...

Running through the hallway of the main floor, "Come on, Franklin!" Emily called the kitten. "We have to find her!" Their frequent games of hide and seek were forever etched in Kathleen's memory.

She was full of life, and her laughter made even Dr. Young smile.

"This isn't a playground." He stood in the doorway of his office and tried to appear firm, but could never keep a straight face. He was wrapped around her finger—she had that affect on the entire staff. Nobody could resist when Emily asked them to hide for her, and even Ian had hidden a few times, thinking his subordinates never knew.

Her loss was tragic, leaving a hopeless feeling for those who had come to know and love her. Her laughter ringing through the main floor was greatly missed, but no one missed her like her father. He tried to manage, but one month after the burial in their native Snowdonia Mountains, he ended his torment with a bottle of sleeping pills.

Outweighing me considerably, Jacob held me beneath him. "You really should've left this alone." His eyes projected the rage of a man with nothing more to lose, a man who had destroyed what was most precious to him.

"A murderer's tormented conscience will drive him to the grave." I quoted The Bible, hoping to appeal to any remaining degree of sanity.

Surprised, he quickly responded, "Proverbs," then continued. "Repent of your sins and turn to God, for the Kingdom of Heaven is near." Without emotion, "Matthew," he finished, then suddenly tried to shove me from the tracks.

I threw a knee into his side, catching him off guard. And with his fingers wrapped for an instant over the edge of the slats, *I have to push him,* I thought. Before he could regain himself I sprang forward, sending him over the edge.

Stunned, he instinctively reached at me and was able to catch my right ankle, causing me to fall to my back. Spinning, I held onto the cold metal track.

"Pull me up," he demanded. "Pull me up or you'll go with me." Then he was silent, realizing that if I reached for him, we'd both fall.

Struggling to keep a hold on the rail, "I can't save you," I yelled. "Let go."

And as I started to lose my grip, Jacob, in a final act of mercy, released me and fell quietly to the rocks below.

A surge went through me. There was hope. But when I tried to regain my hold, I knew it was too late. Splinters shot into my palms as my hands slid across the wooden planks and over sharp pieces of coal.

Intrigued by Elijah's sudden willingness to communicate, Annie closely examined one of his drawings. "This one," she asked, "Where is it?"

"Home," he replied directly.

She leaned closer and noticed recent detail in Elijah's drawing of the train bridge. Frowning, she studied the two prone figures he'd placed on the riverbed beneath the overpass. "When did you do this?" she asked, but he remained silent, waiting for her reaction. "I just don't remember these being here," she pointed to the additions under the coal bridge, and when he still didn't reply, she used a more commanding tone. "Elijah, are these new?"

Noticeably uneasy, "Yes," the boy answered, turning to face her.

"Are they sleeping?"

"No," he said and flinched several times. "No." He then stood and retrieved a drawing from the stack. Putting the incomplete rendering of Goforth's Crossing on the table in front of him, he sat down. Solemnly viewing the page, Elijah's fingers trembled as though resisting the call of the pencil he finally grasped.

Ignoring the commotion in the hallway, he drew Leah on the far side of the covered bridge. It was time for him to sacrifice for the sister who had sacrificed so much for him.

"It's okay," he said, hoping his twin was now happy.

"What's okay?" Annie asked.

When he failed to respond, she turned curiously back to his rendering of the train bridge. The new additions were disturbing, and when she leaned forward for a better look a dire thought came over her.

"Elijah, are these people you know?" When he didn't reply, she faced him, and he began rocking. He wanted no part of the question.

"Elijah? Who are they?"

Finally, he answered. "Jacob."

"Your father?"

"Yes."

"And the other?" Annie cringed. "Who's the other one?" She recognized the face.

— — —

Leah looked over her shoulder, to The Rise of Lanrete Efil, so close, but out of reach. Uncertain. Defeated. She turned to Kris. "So what now?"

"Take my hand," he said.

And when she wrapped her fingers in his, the scenery abruptly changed. The golden grass was gone, as were the purple stones.

They stood on a gravel road, only steps away from Goforth's Crossing, and the sudden change brought her to her knees.

Confused, she stared through the span, then rose to her feet.

"Another bridge? When will this end? You said the other one was the last one."

"But you didn't cross the other one," he answered.

In her dream, she'd been shown compassion that was

often denied in life, and she remembered it all—every step, every moment, and every bridge that she'd spanned to be here at her final crossing.

Fearing that her return would only lead back to the continued scarring of her body and spirit, "What if I'm not ready, or don't wanna go back?" she asked.

"Oh, I think you want to. I think you've *always* wanted to," Kris answered. "And many things will be different," he added, understanding the emotions that kept her from returning, even for the brother she loved more than anything.

In some strange way, it seemed too easy. *Is this it? Can it really be this simple?* She felt like Dorothy, finding she'd always had the power to return home.

"But why am I so scared?"

"Don't be. Just remember the rules."

"Oh yeah, the rules," she mimicked. "But what are they now? They change all the time."

"Is that right? Then only one more rule, okay?"

"Okay," she agreed.

Dropping to one knee, he pulled her close. "Just live," he whispered.

———

"Nooooo...." I screamed. *Is this really happening? I'll wake up before I hit the rocks.*

But I knew I wouldn't wake up. It was no dream, I was free-falling from Elijah's bridge.

When I hit, a surge went through my spine. Paralyzed, battered, I could feel no pain, only the rush of warm blood pouring from the back of my head onto the cold rocks.

Beside me, Jacob was dead. With an expression of relief, he seemed grateful that his misery was over.

One thing was certain—the Reverend Goforth would never give another sermon.

— — —

After a few steps, Leah turned and ran back, throwing her arms around him. "Thank you," she said with a child's sincerity.

"You have to go now. This is your last bridge, and the sun's almost gone. Go, child."

Afraid of leaving the safety of her self-imposed asylum, she trembled, then turned once more to Kris. Unsure of what she might find beyond Goforth's Crossing—her portal back to consciousness—she put her right foot forward.

"Go Dorothy. Go back to Kansas. Run back to Kansas, child!"

With tearful eyes, "Just don't forget about my pass," she said. "Okay?"

"I won't. Now go... Hurry."

Closing her eyes, she thought of her twin, and then bolted like a medalist across the bridge.

Carried by a current on the other side, her feet never touched the ground as she floated above the trail leading to the red brick building.

Elijah, she thought. *Elijah, I'm back.*

He was silent, unresponsive.

I know you're mad.

I'm not mad, he said. *Why would I be mad?*

It was for your own good. I know you don't believe that...

For my own good? Are you kidding me? You said you didn't want me there.

With just a faint glow of light in the west, she went around the back corner and placed her hands on the bricks. And with a slight push, she stepped through the wall, into Elijah's room.

I'm sorry. I am, she said. *But the sun's almost gone, and I don't have time to explain. Come to my room tonight.*

Okay, he answered, now certain which side of the bridge to put her on.

He then erased his sister from behind the bridge, and brought her to the foreground, where he added detail to her face, hair and clothing.

— — —

From the fortress where she'd remained since her father's suicide, Emily stared into the Nevaeh darkness.

"Limbo." It's what Kris had called her voluntary confinement.

To save her father's soul she had waited for Leah, and now she waited for him. Anticipating his arrival, she smiled when a silhouette appeared in the south.

From the depths of damnation, Vaughn Llewellyn approached.

"He's here! He's finally here!" Radiant, filled with life, Emily turned around.

"You've done what you had to do," Kris said. "And did it with grace, Your Majesty." He grinned, recalling her frequent reminders that she was royalty.

Through the corridor, and down the spiral stone staircase, she ran straight to the courtyard, then sprang from stone to stone until she was close enough to see him. And when she saw him, she stopped.

Vaughn looked as if he had been through hell—and he had—but the light in his eyes was reignited the instant he recognized his daughter.

"Emily?" He asked. "Is that you? Is it really you, girl?"

"Yes. It's me." Smiling, she ran to the embrace of her father, with whom she would spend eternity on Mount Epoh Sevil.

Karen reached for the blanket to cover Leah's lifeless body. "Oh my God, Doctor Scott."

Turning to a series of faint heartbeats moving across the monitor, the two watched in disbelief as it abruptly lit up. Like Roman Candles, the signals burst across the screen.

"My God," Kathleen said. "She's off the chart."

Taking a small wrist between her fingers, "She has a pulse," Karen confirmed.

Several staff members came into Leah's room, while others to the window, all of them watching and listening intently to every utterance coming from the child's bedside.

"Dr. Scott, her fingers!" Karen shouted, and those in the room stared in amazement as the child, having been dormant for so long, moved her hand as though reaching for life.

Drawn to the commotion, Kris arched his neck in an effort to get a glimpse of what was happening.

Kathleen, with two fingers held to her lips in disbelief, glanced into the faces of everyone in the room, looking for someone. Turning finally to the window, she held eye contact with Kris. She then went directly to him, and took his arm. "Talk to her. Just come in and *talk* to her." The others stepped aside, and Karen pulled up the chair on which he'd spent many hours.

Cupping her small hand in his, he began. "Dorothy, it's time now." As the staff curiously watched, he whispered, "No worries, child. Just come back." Leaning closer, "Elijah... oh, he misses you, girl," he said. "He needs you here, and many things will be different. It's time now, time to come back to Kansas."

When Leah opened her eyes, a collective gasp was heard throughout the third floor.

She was awake, but was her mind intact? Everyone fell silent, waiting for signs of motor skills.

It took her eyes a moment to adjust to the room light, but once she was able to focus she turned to see whose hand was clutching hers.

Laughter and joyful tears followed as Meadowsview embraced the moment that Leah smiled and whispered, "Scarecrow."

The chopper flew just above the treeline, following the canyon below.

Looking at the map, "Get ready for a bridge up here,"

Helen said.

"How far up?" the pilot asked.

"It shouldn't be much further. After a bend to the left, maybe a half mile more. There," she pointed to the old bridge used to haul coal through the West Virginia mountains.

Desperate, I tried to keep my eyes open, knowing that when they closed, it would be for the last time. But the effort was futile. Ultimately, my eyelids, weighted with fate, fell shut, and I was cast into darkness.

This is it... I'm sorry. I really wanted to keep that promise.

I thought of Kathleen—her smile, green eyes, twisting her hair... If only I had stayed.

Echoing through the gorge, a helicopter was getting louder, closer. Within seconds it sounded as if it was almost directly overhead, and I tried again to open my eyes.

By nothing less than the grace of God, I was able to open them enough for a final view of Elijah's bridge.

Lani had returned, and for a moment she was lit by the chopper's spotlight. Holding something, she was angelic, at peace.

When she released the Mylar balloon we both watched it spiral upward, higher and higher, until it was only a spec that vanished in the blackness.

Chapter 17

The headstones were aligned in west-facing rows on several hills overlooking the ocean. Autumn had all but completely stripped many of the the trees, causing them to appear vulnerable. But *nothing* could be more vulnerable than Kathleen. In disbelief, she clutched John's arm as they followed the others to the freshly dug grave.

"How could this happen?"

"I don't know," he answered. "Everything was taking off for him. Then, out of the blue... he's gone."

"I feel like I'm to blame." She looked at him with red eyes, weak from crying.

"You didn't tell him to go to Huntington. He could've just come home. That's what I don't understand. Why did he change flights? How the hell did he end up on a bridge in West Virginia?"

"For Leah. The twins. He did it for the them."
"Wait. The twins? What twins?"
"We'll talk when this is over."

Dressed in black, the immediate family was seated on one side of the casket, and to her surprise John led Kathleen to the front.

"No, she whispered. "That's for family."

"There's a chair for you," he responded.

"I've known David since he was a boy. He and John made the best paper airplanes I'd ever seen." Smiling, the old Baptist minister recalled the Weston boys disrupting his Sunday School class.

"Like some of you, I watched him grow up. And like *each* of you, I've tried to find reason for his death. But we're not here to question God's will, we're here to remember David Michael Weston's life."

The eulogy, twenty minutes of prayer and scriptures, gave Kathleen little consolation. Beside her, John was equally distraught, trying to keep his composure.

"Please bow your heads. God, we ask that you commend David's spirit into Your open arms, and that a place be made in Your house. Today, we remember our friend, our brother." He looked at John—who broke into tears—and continued. "There will be many times when we will miss him, but today let us remember how David made us smile. His quick wit or that mischievous grin. And when you remember him, don't think of how he died—think of how he lived and touched your heart."

When it was over, the gathering slowly thinned until John and Kathleen were the only ones there.

"Are you okay?" he asked.

"Yes," she answered. "I just... I think I'll take a walk."

"Want some company?"

"No," she said. "I mean..."

"I know what you mean. And it's okay."

"I just need a few minutes alone."

"Take as long as you want."

"Thanks," she whispered and turned to the west.

The Pacific, vast and empty, had never looked as gray, and as she put her first foot forward, *Let me wake up,* she thought. *Let it all be nothing but a dream. It's only a dream.*

Kathleen walked down the hill, toward evergreens lining both sides of a narrow stream. Entering the grove, she came to a wooden bench and recalled a similar bench, one where she and David sat only a few days before she left for New England...

"You could find something here, I'm sure," he'd said.

"I know. But dad called in a lot of favors to get me this position, and it's one of the best hospitals of its kind. It's a good opportunity. One I can't pass."

"I'm just saying, LA has plenty of good hospitals—Children's, right here, UCLA's one of the best anywhere."

"I've met with the big boss. It's a done deal. But why now? I mean, seriously. You wait til I'm leaving to ask me to stay?"

"I'm not asking you to stay."

"Well, it sure sounds like it."

"I'm just saying... I guess I never really thought about you leaving." He tried to seem indifferent, but she could tell he'd miss her as much as she'd miss him.

Kathleen stared at the trees, but didn't see them. Nothing made sense—even God's will.

With bloodshot eyes, she stood and started to walk back to his grave, and had she not turned around she would've missed it, but something caused her to look back.

In disbelief, at first she thought it was only her imagination...

A Monarch butterfly flew above the stream, then another, and another. Before long there were hundreds, a silent swarm migrating to its winter home. Orange and black, ardent wings fluttered southward, against a mild crosswind from the west.

In two distinct rows, they followed the age-old path to La Jolla.

Kathleen fell to her knees and took a handful of leaves. *Damn it, David,* she thought, and crushed them in her palm.

Laughing and crying at once, she fell apart.

This day, this moment, would become a memory that would never fade.

But it wasn't supposed to be this way. She flung the powdery leaves into the wind. *It wasn't supposed to end this way. What am I supposed to do now?*

Watching until only the stragglers remained, when the

last of them was gone, she stared vacantly at the scenery.

"What am I supposed to do now?" she whispered.

Soon...

When? Elijah asked. *You said soon yesterday.*

She'll be back soon, Leah thought. *Tomorrow. She'll be here tomorrow.*

Bored with her view of the meadow, she faced the door. Alert. Restless. She wasn't planning to stay in her room much longer.

Where is she? he asked.

She turned again to the window and closed her eyes...

She's telling him goodbye, she finally answered. *They're saying goodbye.*

Printed in Great Britain
by Amazon